T0007762

The Unknown Stigma

2

〈The Resurrection〉

IRH Press

BOOKS

IRH PRESS

New York

ISBN 13: 978-1-942125-28-0

ISBN 10: 1-942125-28-3

Printed in Japan

First Edition

Cover Image: shutterstock / wandee007

The Unknown Stigma

2

〈The Resurrection〉

Ryuho Okawa

IRH PRESS

1.

How far did I soar up into the sky?

St. Agnes was ascending with Detective Yuri Okada, but she lost the detective along the way. It was around the sixth dimensional Light Realm, where all sorts of experts got together. Higher up in that realm, there also seemed to be ethnic gods who could be regarded as "local deities."

St. Agnes, however, kept ascending through one, two, and three transparent screens that were not visible to the naked eye until she finally reached a world called the Bodhisattva Realm of the seventh dimension. The inside of the white iron fencing that looked like the premises of a foreign embassy was filled with roses of all colors in full bloom. The central gate opened. White fog was drifting over the ground, to a little above her knees.

When St. Agnes entered the gate, 10 or so sisters came out to greet her.

Unveiling the Secret
of
The Unknown Stigma,

VISIT

https://okawabooks.com/the-unknown-stigma

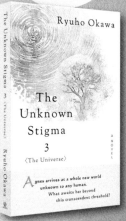

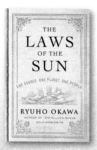
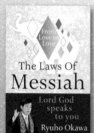
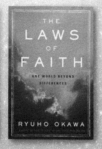
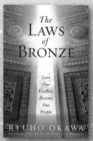

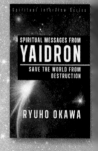

They escorted her into the reception room inside a guest house. It was a white-themed room, and there was a vase on a marble table, with neatly arranged red, yellow, and white roses.

The door opened and, unexpectedly, Mother Teresa came in. Mother Teresa, known as the Saint of India, founded a hospice in Calcutta called *Home for the Dying* and passed away quite a while ago. St. Agnes at least knew this much.

"Agnes, you have done well. We were cheering for you from here, the seventh dimension."

"You're Mother Teresa, right? My soul is not worthy to be invited to such a place. I'm quite sinful, and I've killed people too. Perhaps you were sent as a priestess to hear my confession," Agnes said.

"No, I wasn't. I had you stop by because I wanted to meet you," Mother Teresa said.

"Will my sins be forgiven?"

"I just want you to make yourself comfortable

here, as Jesus asked me to do. I appreciate your hard work."

As soon as Mother Teresa finished her sentence, there was a knock at the door, and another sister walked in with Darjeeling tea, white muffins, and strawberry jam.

"Oh, thank you. But if I may, isn't it strange for a dead person like me to be eating or drinking?" Agnes asked.

"You've only recently left the human world," said Sister Martha. "So you should still have physical senses. You'll be able to taste the tea and the muffin."

"Get some rest, and prepare for your next journey," said Mother Teresa.

"Isn't this convent here going to be my nunnery? I won't be living here?" Agnes asked.

"No, you'd better meet with a higher being and receive guidance for your future plans," Mother Teresa answered.

"But I still haven't received a final judgment from His Excellency Archbishop of Tokyo Ignatius on whether I'm endowed with God's power or the devil's power."

"I like your humility," said Mother Teresa. "But you were only halfway through your mission. You were caught in a terrible battle, weren't you? All right, dear. Once you get some rest, head over to see Jesus. I'm the head of this nunnery, so I'm afraid I can't accompany you."

"How will I be able to see Jesus Christ?"

"You have white wings on your shoulders, you see? Those wings will carry you," Mother Teresa said.

Only now did Agnes realize that she had large wings of angels coming out of her shoulders, just like in the paintings at St. Peter's Basilica. Her entire body was wrapped in a white, lacy, holy robe. Her chest had stopped bleeding.

"You're the only sister who was given a cross-shaped stigma from Jesus. You must learn more about who you really are."

Having said so, Mother Teresa left the room. After a brief moment, the nunnery started to fade away like a mirage. One sister who was left in the garden said, "Alright, this way," as she pointed her finger toward the sky.

Agnes' wings on her shoulders started to flap up and down. Once again, she flew past three thin transparent screens and entered a world where golden trees grew out of silver sand.

It was the eighth dimensional Tathagata Realm, a world where religious saints from various religions such as Christianity, Buddhism, Islam, Taoism, Hinduism, and Japanese Shinto had a good time walking around and speaking with each other.

Out came a brother who introduced himself as Francis of Assisi. He was wrapped in a black church uniform, and there was a halo-like golden ring behind his head.

"Agnes, follow me," Francis said.

He held her right hand with his left hand and ascended even higher. Again, they passed through a thin, transparent dimensional screen, then another, until they finally landed after the third screen.

There, Jesus Christ greeted Agnes. It was as if he came out of a ring of light. Jesus placed two fingers of his right hand on top of her head and blessed Agnes.

"I shall take you to the Lord God. This is an occasion like no other."

As he said so, Jesus took Agnes past the burning, fire-like wall of the ninth dimension. Agnes found herself bowing down before the throne.

Jesus Christ spoke.

"Here is Lord God. He is sometimes called

Alpha, Elohim, or El Cantare."

Agnes could not directly gaze at the Lord. It was as if the palace was made of diamond.

The Lord spoke.

"Agnes, your mission is yet to be over. You shall resurrect."

It all felt like a dream. What would happen next?

"You're one of the four Seraphim," the voice echoed.

2.

"AHHH," Agnes screamed as she began to fall sharply. She was getting dizzy.

She realized that a beautiful white-looking angel with golden hair, not distinctly male or female, was escorting her from the right side.

"I am Archangel Gabriel. I received an order to guard you going forth." The voice echoed inside her heart like a telepathic message. He turned out to be a young male angel, probably around the age of 30.

"By Archangel Gabriel, you mean *the* Gabriel in the Annunciation to the Virgin Mary?"

"If that makes it easier for you to understand, you can think like that. I also serve as a messenger who bridges the heavenly world and the earthly world."

Soon after Gabriel said so, they pierced through the clouds and the earthly world came into sight.

Agnes saw Camp Ichigaya of the Self-Defense Forces of Tokyo. Fire trucks had hosed down the place, and the fire seemed to have died out.

She descended into the room where the last battle was fought. Agnes, in the form of an angel, saw her dead body that had stopped breathing. The bodies of the people from the First Criminal Investigation Division, the Self-Defense Forces, and the Ministry of Defense were also lying around. She was not sure whether they were dead or alive. She saw the blood streaming out of the chest of her corpse fade away and the bullet hole on her chest close up. Then, she realized that a thin, silver thread had stemmed out from the back of her corpse's head, and it was connected to the head of herself in the form of an angel. In only a second, Agnes' spiritual body was sucked back into her physical body.

Her eyes snapped open.

"Anyway, I have to get out of here."

Saying so, she got up and ran out of the room. The site was so chaotic that no one tried to stop her from leaving. Rather, the air was tense because people were anxious that they would be hit by a second intercontinental ballistic missile (ICBM).

Agnes fled to the nearest town. She had nowhere to go.

"That's right; I'll somehow find a way to get to Set-chan's apartment."

Set-chan was hired as a bar proprietress at Tachibana, a hostess bar in Gotanda. She claimed herself to be Setsuko Nikaido, taking after a Japanese actress named Fumi Nikaido. Surely, there was a slight resemblance between the actress and Set-chan.

Agnes did not want to be treated as a suspect again, so she decided to use her made-up secular name, Suzu Nomura. She went up to the second floor of a cheap-looking apartment building and pounded on the door of room 205. Setsuko came out.

"Hey, what time do you think it is?"

Setsuko looked a bit grumpy, but a visitor at half past midnight was not really a nuisance for someone working at a hostess bar.

"Oh my, it's Suzu," Setsuko said after she opened the door.

"Well, come on in."

"Thank you."

It was a while since Suzu last visited this old apartment.

"All of a sudden, you ran away, and all of a sudden, you're back," Setsuko said.

"I didn't know where else to go."

"Did the cops get you?"

"That sounds about right."

"You've got soot stains all over your clothes

and your face is so dirty. You look just like Jean Valjean from *Les Misérables*, who made an underground escape."

"Can't you at least compare me to Cosette, the daughter?"

"Go wash up, and then I'll call you Cosette. You're ruining your pretty face looking like this."

Suzu Nomura took a shower. Both the bullet mark and the blood on her chest were gone, although her cross-shaped bruise remained.

When Suzu came out of the shower wrapped in a bath towel, she saw a pair of pajamas that Setsuko had prepared for her. Setsuko was about two inches taller than Suzu, so her strawberry-patterned pajamas were large and loose enough. Suzu felt at ease.

"I won't tell anyone. Which prison did you run from?" Setsuko asked.

"I escaped Camp Ichigaya of Self-Defense Forces, not prison."

"You made the last train?"

"Well, yes."

"They said on TV that North Korea's ICBM fell on the Self-Defense Forces' base. Luckily, it wasn't a nuclear missile, but they say that Tokyo would be ruined if North Korea launched a nuclear missile next. People have already started moving out of Tokyo by car."

"But we have to survive at all costs."

"I don't know much about international affairs, but it looks like Taiwan is responding to a missile attack by China. Our Senkaku Islands were also occupied by China, and they sank five Japan Coast Guard (JCG) vessels. Also, Russian bombers from the Northern Territories bombed Sapporo, and I've heard it's a sea of fire over there."

"It's a mess. People don't know where to run."

"Our Prime Minister Tabata is missing. Who knows what'll happen?"

Setsuko made instant noodles for her, just like last time.

"I want to eat ramen noodles in Sangenjaya again," Suzu quietly said as she slurped the noodles.

Then, large drops of tears ran down Suzu's cheeks. Setsuko was surprised to see that.

She kept silent for a while as she listened to the slurping of instant noodles.

3.

Setsuko made Suzu Nomura rest for a day.

In the afternoon on day two, she made a simple omelet and rice for Suzu while the girl was watching the news on TV. She felt so glad to see Suzu happily eating the omelet with a spoon, showing her white teeth as she smiled.

"Alright, I'm about to tell you something important so listen up," Setsuko said. "Various people have been stopping by Bar Tachibana to investigate—from gangs to cops, the Self-Defense Forces, and the Ministry of Defense. Sometimes we get guys from the U.S. Embassy, the South Korean Embassy, and the Chinese Embassy. They're all like looking for you."

"That's a problem. Maybe I'm on the international wanted list."

"Our manager Aoi is doing a good job dealing with them, and our bartender Imagawa is good at handling gangs. According to what I've heard, the head of that notorious Motoyama Family was completely knocked out by a young girl, who grabbed him by the collar and knocked him against the ceiling. What superhuman strength, huh? The machine gun was twisted like candy, and all the fired bullets drifted away without hitting the target. I mean, this is like *The Matrix*. It's practically Keanu Reeves. Apparently, even their Japanese sword was ripped apart. The surviving gang members are scared, but they're still looking for that young girl. Our manager shoos them away, saying that our fortune-teller, Natalie, can use clairvoyance and receive spiritual messages but that she has never bent a single spoon."

"Sorry for causing you all the trouble."

"But that hoodlum, Goro Ichikawa, was arrested, and he testified that the photo of Natalie reminded him of a high school girl he raped in Nagoya. He was yelling that she went mad and became a monster after the four of them gang-raped her. He said she must be burning with a vengeance. Now that the cops know about the four scums in Nagoya, they seem to be looking into the case. Of course, I didn't say a word about you."

"Then I'll leave the case to the police. I hold absolutely no grudge against anyone right now, and I can only think of that incident as my 'passion of Christ' that helped me grow," Suzu said.

"Wow, you've changed. You seem more 'saint-like.' Wanna get back into fortune-telling?" Setsuko asked.

"Oh no, I'm not sure I can do that again."

"By the way, in the Motoyama Family case, the young girl helped the officers from the First Criminal Investigation Division quite a lot, but after the Self-Defense Forces took her away, they too seem to have gone missing," Setsuko said.

"They are over at Camp Ichigaya, either dead or injured."

"Is that where the ICBM exploded?"

"It was the first time that I saw a battle between the Self-Defense Forces and the First Criminal Investigation Division," Suzu said.

"Okay. I kind of understand how things went down. But you may not be able to escape for even a week because the Public Security Bureau is looking for you and the whatever-bureau of the Ministry of Defense also wants to capture you."

"Um, do you know anything about Taneda, my father?" Suzu asked.

"He seems to be hospitalized, so you shouldn't see him right now. It'll cause trouble for the family, and I bet the authorities are on a stakeout nearby."

Suzu started to understand the situation she was placed in.

"Maybe I should turn myself over to the church."

"If you are a female 'Keanu Reeves,' I'm sure the church will demonize you and confine you somewhere in their nunnery. Don't go now."

"What am I supposed to do then?"

"At this rate, whoever gets you first between the Public Security Bureau and the Ministry of Defense wins. There's a guy I know, Mr. Onuki, who runs a religion-based talent production company. He might be able to help you," Setsuko said.

Onuki was supposed to visit them the following day, but Setsuko's telephone line had already been wiretapped by the Public Security Bureau.

Thirty minutes later, 20 members of the Special Attack Team surrounded Setsuko's apartment. Suzu calmly turned herself over to them so as not to cause Setsuko any trouble.

A secure bus with windows that were protected by iron bars took her to the Metropolitan Police Department.

St. Agnes, a.k.a. Suzu Nomura, was to be investigated at the Metropolitan Police Department yet again. The Public Security Bureau and the First Criminal Investigation Division's special team formed a temporary co-op alliance.

Director Jiro Sugisaki and Director Kenichi Nakayama of the First Criminal Investigation Division, who survived the incident, were relieved to have secured Agnes.

Director Anzai of the Public Security Bureau also wanted to solve the latest mystery case.

They found out what had happened to Team Yamasaki. The only person who could return to duty was Detective Mitsuru Noyama from Nagoya. Everyone else had little chance of survival.

They also found out about the deaths of the Ministry of Defense's director general for special missions, Hideki Takahashi, and Director Mitsuo Maejima as well as the death of Takao Hirose, chief of staff of the Air Self-Defense Force.

They had to find a way to cover up the deaths and clean up the aftermath in a seamless manner. After that, the only thing left for them would be to figure out what to do with Agnes' special powers and the war.

4.

Kenichi Nakayama, director of the First Criminal Investigation Division, and Nobuyuki Anzai, director of the Public Security Bureau, decided to conduct an unusual joint investigation into the supernatural powers of Agnes, a.k.a. Suzu Nomura.

"Anyway," Nakayama said, "we need to find out what kinds of supernatural powers she has and how powerful they are. Depending on that, we must utilize her powers extralegally as secret weapons of our country, like the Ministry of Defense says."

"If she uses her true power, our handguns won't work on her. She can probably remotely turn us into corpses. We have no choice but to treat her politely and ask her to cooperate with us," Anzai agreed.

"As for the person-in-charge, our division will appoint Chief Naoyuki Yamane," Nakayama said. "He's a former Secret Service agent, so his skills in judo, kendo, karate, shooting, arresting techniques, whatever-you-name-it, are through the roof. Besides, he's a knockout that looks like the actor, Yama-Pi, Tomohisa Yamashita, so Agnes would hesitate to kill him. Hopefully, she'll become like his girlfriend and be a secret weapon of the Metropolitan Police."

"Then we'll appoint Chief Haruka Kazami on our end. She graduated from the University of Tokyo, and she's sharp-minded. She is also good at reading people's minds, so she should be able to take care of Agnes' feelings. This girl looks like the actress Haruka Ayase, and she could even be an action actress. We call her 'Haruka Ayase of the Public Security Bureau,'" Anzai said.

"That'll do. Let's use those two and send in extra support if needed."

Now, Chiefs Naoyuki Yamane and Haruka Kazami were facing Agnes in a room, while

Director Sugisaki, Director Nakayama of the First Criminal Investigation Division, and Anzai, director of the Public Security Bureau, watched across the one-way mirror.

Chief Yamane was the first to open his mouth. He had a crisp facial expression, and he could even pass for a businessman of a top-notch trading company.

"Ms. Agnes. Currently, the whereabouts of Prime Minister Tabata is unknown. Do you know where he is?"

"He's hiding in a management office of the underground water storage near the Metropolitan Government Building in Shinjuku out of fear of a nuclear missile attack," Agnes answered.

"And you can see that?"

"Yes, I can see it vividly when I concentrate my thoughts."

"What is the prime minister up to?"

"He has set up several small TVs to keep a

close watch on the situation. He seems to be communicating with others through paper memos because he is afraid that a phone call might be intercepted by foreign spies."

"So that means he's alright for now."

"I also see an attending doctor and two nurses by his side. The other five people must be from the Secret Service."

Wow. She is something! Chief Yamane shouted in his head.

"What will happen to Japan?" Kazami asked.

"The future will be created by many people's thoughts and actions, so I won't be able to tell you. But there's no doubt this is the biggest crisis since this country was founded."

"I guess we the police can't do much anymore," Kazami said.

"Well, I think the Public Security Bureau can at least block out the spies from China, Russia, and North Korea who have infiltrated into Japan.

Now that the U.S. president was assassinated, the CIA is also actively investigating."

"What?! The U.S. president was assassinated?" Yamane and Kazami shouted together in shock.

"No TV channels or newspapers have reported it yet," said Agnes. "But President Obamiden was assassinated by small drone missiles while he was playing golf. And now, Vice President Deborah, a Black woman, is the acting president."

"That's a serious concern for Japan's defense," Kazami said.

"Was the assassin an American? Or a foreign terrorist?" Yamane asked.

"The mastermind behind the scenes is Russian President Rasputin, who believes the U.S. president set him up in the Ukrainian War, but the perpetrators are terrorists handpicked from Latin American immigrants."

"No wonder the Ministry of Defense wants this girl more than we do," Kazami said.

"But when I think about Team Yamasaki's mortification, I definitely want to take care of Agnes here at the Metropolitan Police Department," Yamane said.

"Chief Yamasaki was shot with 10 machine gun bullets even though he held up his police badge," Agnes said. "He wouldn't have survived even if he had worn a bulletproof vest. As for Detective Doman Yogiashi, a bullet penetrated his left eye. Even the art of *onmyodo*, the way of yin and yang, may not be enough to save him. Detective Mitsuru Noyama was hit by two bullets on his right thigh, but he should be able to make a comeback if the bullets didn't go through his bones."

"What happened to Detective Yuri Okada?" Kazami asked.

"She ascended with me through the Spirit World, but I lost sight of her along the way."

"So you're saying that you, too, had died with her?"

"That seems to be the case, but I was miraculously revived," Agnes answered.

"Are you immortal? Maybe you're like Wolverine," Yamane said.

"Um, I don't think that's a good example. In my case, there's more of a religious meaning."

"So you're saying that yours was like the resurrection of Jesus Christ," Kazami said.

"Yes, Jesus himself helped me as well."

"It's no surprise for St. Agnes, huh?" Yamane said. "How 'bout I recognize you as a saint instead of the Vatican. Say, if I were shot to death, can you bring me back to life?"

"If there is love," answered Agnes.

"What does that mean?"

"If you're a nasty man, die off. That's what she means," Kazami said.

"Ouch," Yamane said.

That was the end of the day's interview. The officers who had been watching across the one-way mirror felt that Agnes' powers had to be reported to the cabinet minister via the superintendent general and the commissioner general of the National Police Agency.

It was decided that Agnes would sleep in a special room within the Metropolitan Police Department for the time being.

5.

That night, Agnes had a dream. Okinawa was on fire. The deck-shaped airfield at Henoko's maritime base was heavily damaged by submarine-launched missiles. The Osprey helicopters were either set aflame or overturned, so no soldiers could be sent to the Senkaku Islands. The Chinese army was steadily building a fortified base for missiles on the Islands.

Eight JCG vessels approached the Islands and gave a warning in Chinese. But nearly 3,000 Chinese fishing boats were scattered in the sea, and missile drones that flew from these boats attacked the JCG ships one by one, sinking them into the sea.

Five Maritime Self-Defense Force destroyers arrived in a flurry near the Senkaku Islands from Sasebo, but they were hit by 500 missiles from the hastily built missile base on the islands. Three destroyers sank, and two were wrecked. Japan couldn't fight back because there was no order from the prime minister, the head of the civilian control of the Self-Defense Forces.

Three anti-submarine warfare helicopters were also shot down by rocket launchers from Chinese fishing boats.

Ten jets of the Fleet Air Wing 31 scrambled from Iwakuni and shot down two Chinese jets, but the Japanese jets were all shot down by the *Yamatano Orochi*-modified missiles—China's new weapon in which one missile splits into eight smaller missiles to chase down the target.

A globe-encircling nuclear missile dropped on the Futenma base, where the main U.S. military units remained, and the resulting flames painted the night sky red. The nuclear missile that circled Earth at Mach 20 came flying from the direction of Australia. The missile was intended to isolate Taiwan, which was attacked along with the Senkaku Islands. Japan's Self-Defense Forces were unable to protect its own country, and Prime Minister Tabata could not keep the diplomatic promise he had made with Taiwan to defend them in case they were attacked.

It went without saying that the United States was also unsettled. President Obamiden's death was still concealed, so the government couldn't issue military orders.

Before she knew it, Agnes' dream was directed to the Korean Peninsula.

Nuclear missiles were fired from five locations in North Korea, and they were aimed at South Korea's five major cities. Seoul was a sea of fire. The nuclear missile that was aimed at Seoul landed in a matter of 10 minutes, so the U.S. interceptor system did not work. North Korea called for South Korea to surrender on its Pyongyang Broadcasting Station. However, South Korea's Blue House was already hit by North Korea's nuclear missile, so there was no one to negotiate with Pyongyang. The Pyongyang Broadcasting Station called for about 600,000 South Korean soldiers to surrender. They also announced that tomorrow won't come for the U.S. military base stationed in Japan because North Korea, along with China and Russia, had fired nuclear missiles all at once.

In Japan, the U.S. military bases and Self-Defense Forces' bases were the main targets under attack. The defense minister had returned to her hometown in the Osaka metropolitan district, but the bullet train was already suspended and airports were so heavily destroyed that neither JAL nor ANA, the two biggest airlines in Japan, were operating. The broadcast pirating was so intense that the defense minister couldn't get in touch with Tokyo.

Power outages occurred one after another in major Japanese cities. Japan had been serious in its effort to turn away from fossil fuels, and almost all the nuclear power plants were out of operation. Solar panels were bombed one after another by foreign spies residing in Japan. Natural gas from Russia had stopped coming in.

The Metropolitan Police Department, where Agnes was located, also experienced power blackouts from time to time, so they switched to in-house power generation.

Perhaps not everything Agnes was seeing in her dream was real. But it must be a continuation of ongoing reality. After all, even the TV was no longer working.

After being attacked by North Korea, Russia, and China, Prime Minister Tabata went into hiding in fear of missiles, Agnes thought. *The president of the United States is dead. The vice president's political abilities are doubtful. But if the U.S. military bases in Japan were attacked with nuclear weapons, the United States will surely make counterattacks from the mainland U.S., Hawaii, and Guam even if they cannot obtain a United Nations resolution. I can only do what I can.*

The night turned to day as Agnes had these thoughts.

The major newspapers in Japan—*Asahi*, *Yomiuri*, *Nikkei*, *Sankei*, *Mainichi*, and *Tokyo*—were under attack. None were able to publish their morning newspapers.

Tokyo Sports, *Daily Sports*, *Nikkan Sports*, and *Nikkan Gendai* were circulating in the Metropolitan Police Department, but not one newspaper had any clue what was happening around Japan and the rest of the world.

A hypersonic missile out of rage from Russia hit NHK, Japan's public broadcaster, and they went up in flames. A missile from China hit Nippon Television, and two Scud-like missiles from an unidentified submarine in the Pacific

Ocean hit Fuji Television. The two broadcasting stations, Nippon Television and Fuji Television, were on fire. The people of Japan closely listened to the radio, but there was so much conflicting information. It was left to the United States and the European Union (E.U.) to respond to the situation.

After a simple breakfast, Agnes was turned over to the Ministry of Defense.

Vice-Minister of Defense for International Affairs Manobe came over, along with Assistant Director Kazumi Suzumoto who was working as a secretary, to pick her up. A black car headed from the Metropolitan Police Department near Sakurada-mon Gate to the Ministry of Defense through the streets of Tokyo—now a city pitch black in smoke.

6.

Agnes was facing Manobe in the vice-minister's office within the Ministry of Defense. The man had a slender body for someone in such a stern government office, and his grave eyes behind his black-rimmed spectacles glistened as if he were trying to see through the truth.

"You've seen how Tokyo was this morning. How do you feel?" Manobe asked.

"I've never experienced a real war. All I'm thinking about is what I can do in this situation," Agnes answered.

She looked out the window toward the Imperial Palace. The forest was on fire.

"The Imperial Palace has a safe underground shelter, so you need not worry," Manobe explained. "Our prime minister is hiding deep underground for fear of atomic and hydrogen bombs, so Chief Cabinet Secretary Koichi Mamiya is taking charge. Our female defense minister, Takasugi, has been stuck in the Osaka metropolitan district and hasn't made her usual hawkish speech yet. Both the senior vice-minister of defense and the vice-minister of defense are on standby at their homes, so I am temporarily responsible for making major decisions within the Ministry."

"I don't know a great deal about the organizational structure of government offices. Please let me know if there's anything I can do for you. How much of the Self-Defense Forces is functioning?" Agnes asked.

"We still have about 80% of our military capabilities. But as you know, Japan is under a simultaneous attack from North Korea, Russia, and China, and we are still unsure of our defensive strategy."

Just then, Assistant Director Kazumi Suzumoto entered the room and served tea. She sat down to join in on the conversation.

"Ms. Suzumoto, what's your role?" Agnes asked.

"I was asked to support you, Ms. Agnes, in any way that I can. It could be more comfortable for you to talk with another woman," Suzumoto said.

Suzumoto looked four or five years older than Agnes. She had studied abroad and was hired as a high-ranking bureaucrat after graduating from Keio University's Faculty of Law.

"Let's start with defending against North Korea because they're not capable of fighting a lengthy battle," Agnes suggested.

"You're right," Manobe agreed. "We can't do anything about China and Russia unless the United States does something."

"North Korea will launch another ICBM in the next hour. It will be aimed at the Tokyo metropolitan district," Agnes said.

"But there are 40 million people living here," Suzumoto said.

"That's why we need to make sure it doesn't hit the ground."

"But how?" Manobe asked.

"I will ask God to change its trajectory."

"I don't mean to doubt you, but is that really possible?" Suzumoto asked.

"The Lord is Almighty. There's nothing the Lord God can't do," Agnes said.

Manobe and Suzumoto looked over at each other.

"Ah, it looks like the ICBM was already fired. It was fired in a lofted trajectory, and it's targeting this building here at the Ministry of Defense," Agnes said.

Even a PAC-3 (Patriot Advanced Capability-3 missile) can't shoot down an ICBM that is launched to an altitude of 3,700 miles before falling. What's more, Camp Ichigaya is no longer functioning after it suffered considerable damage. Could we intercept it from the Yokota Base?

These thoughts ran through Manobe's head.

"No, we don't need a missile to counter their ICBM. I'll pray to God and cast, 'YES, U-turn.'"

Saying so, Agnes kneeled down on both knees and took a posture of prayer. She was not dressed as a sister, but she had on an elegant navy blue suit. That should suffice.

"The ICBM launched from North Korea, you must turn around. Fly toward Mt. Paektu."

She prayed and prayed.

Around 15 minutes had passed when a memo was delivered to Manobe from the chief of staff of the Joint Staff Office: "The ICBM is heading in the opposite direction." Eventually, the ICBM crashed directly into the hillside of Mt. Paektu— the birthplace of North Korea and thus their holy ground.

Mt. Paektu suffered a tremendous explosion. "YES, U-turn" was successful. Volcanic bombs fell heavily on downtown Pyongyang and northeastern China, followed by a mass of ashfall. An abundance of lava flowed out as well. North Korea's nuclear missile site up north was almost ruined by the lava, and likewise, nuclear missile sites in northeastern China were disabled.

Over in Pyongyang, volcanic bombs fell one after another. Five body doubles of General Secretary Kim Show-un died. The real dictator was still hiding in an underground shelter. Almost-a-mile-deep shelter could withstand both atomic and hydrogen bombs, and this shelter had underground passageways stemming out in all directions.

Next, Agnes offered a "Prayer for Great Earthquake" to the Lord God. A magnitude-9.0 earthquake struck right below Pyongyang. Buildings of all sorts collapsed.

Through her special ability of remote view-ing, Agnes herself had already seen the turn of events that was reported to the Ministry of Defense by the Meteorological Agency: the eruption of Mt. Paektu and the resulting magnitude-9.0 epicentral earthquake in Pyongyang. According to the report, they were still confirming whether the earthquake was a real earthquake or a nuclear explosion at an underground shelter.

The Air Self-Defense Force flew the F-35 and confirmed the eruption and smoke coming out of Mt. Paektu along with pyroclastic flows.

"Phew," Agnes let out a long breath.

Manobe and Suzumoto were struck with awe at the immeasurable powers of Agnes.

She's Japan's secret weapon, Manobe thought.

Meanwhile, Suzumoto felt that The-Holy-One was also lending his power. She was think-ing about Japan's no. 1 religious leader who had graduated from the same school as Manobe.

7.

Meanwhile, at the Embassy of Japan in Russia, Japanese Ambassador to Russia Masaru Kamizuki was in agony. Japan–Russia relations were quite amicable when Prime Minister Shinnosuke Ando, the longest-serving prime minister since the 19th century, was in office. The minister of foreign affairs at the time was Saburo Tabata, the current prime minister; Tabata only provided behind-the-scenes support and acted as Ando's "yes-man" because Ando prided himself on his diplomatic endeavors. He sold himself as "Good Listener Tabata" and waited for pennies to fall from heaven.

Ando was friendly enough with President Rasputin to invite the president to a hot spring back near his hometown, and if Ando had another term, Japan and Russia could've signed a peace treaty. Japan was close to signing the peace treaty under the condition that Russia would return the two islands in the Northern Territories to Japan; that Japan would promote its large-scale investment in Siberia and Sakhalin; and that Japan would not exercise the U.S.–Japan military alliance aimed at recapturing the Northern Territories.

The unexpected coronavirus pandemic overturned the situation. U.S. President Donald King had been advocating America's economic recovery and to make America strong again; it was almost certain for him to be reelected, but he ended up losing his presidential ticket owing to a surge in coronavirus cases and an unexpected "ring-side battle" throughout the presidential election. President King was in the midst of investigating Mr. Obamiden's collusion with China, but instead, the media spread Donald's alleged collusion with Russia. The mass media believed that "anti-Donald King" was the only way they could bring back "mass-media democracy," so they backed Obamiden. As a result, although Donald King was elected on Election Day with a record-breaking number of votes, Obamiden won the election after adding up the mail-in ballots that were postmarked by Election Day. The U.S. democracy was in turmoil after the back-and-forth media reports of the candidates' suspected scandals. The coronavirus pandemic, police brutality against the Black community, and the protest at the Capitol also worked against Donald. Consequently, Obamiden, who praised "mass-media democracy," was elected as president. The vice president, a Black woman who seemed to be no different than a member of the Communist Party, was also welcomed by the liberal media. This was how the current president—who was now assassinated but announced to be "hospitalized"—came to power all while his cognitive decline was being suspected.

Donald King and Russian President Rasputin

recognized each other as political geniuses. King even held two miraculous conferences with the third-generation North Korean leader he referred to as "Little Rocket Man," and he became the first U.S. president to enter north of the 38th parallel. When King was infected with the coronavirus, the "Little Rocket Man" sent a telegram wishing King a speedy recovery. King was an exceptionally strong negotiator in the United States; this president would've been worthy of the Nobel Peace Prize.

The United States made a mistake. As President King said, "fake news" media was the mainstream. Moreover, President Obamiden of the Democratic Party cunningly pulled off verbal attacks against Russia while removing suspicions against China as the perpetrator of COVID-19.

Obamiden set a trap for Russia's Rasputin. He began supplying weapons to Ukraine beginning last autumn, effectively bringing Ukraine into the North Atlantic Treaty Organization (NATO) and turning the country into a battleground. Obamiden was also planning for NATO countries to continue supplying weapons to Ukraine until they could get Crimea back and demolish the two separatist regions in eastern Ukraine. Obamiden aimed at bringing back the classic Cold War framework of "democracy vs. autocracy"—all without getting his hands dirty.

Now, the world that has reverted to the Cold War era under the Obamiden strategy began to polarize in a dangerous manner. Russia, China, North Korea, Iran, Syria, and South America started to oppose the West. The ancient saying, "The enemy of my enemy is my friend," revived, and Russia, China, and North Korea began to join hands, although they were reluctant about it. Another difficult matter was whether India would side with the United States or Russia. India had strong military ties with Russia to counter Chinese invasion.

Meanwhile, the Quad (Quadrilateral Security Dialogue) was formed by the United States, Japan, Australia, and India to join forces against China and prevent Chinese ambitions in Asia. But there was a gridlock here, too. The United States lagged behind in the technology of the hypersonic missile, which was already shared among Russia, China, and North Korea. The United States, Japan, and Australia would be able to jointly develop the hypersonic missile by late next year, but whether India would take their side remained uncertain. It felt like ages ago that a crowd of over 100,000 people in India packed a sports stadium and welcomed U.S. President Donald King during his presidency. With such strong distrust in the American two-party system, the implementation of parliamentary democracy and a two-party system into China's politics would be held off further.

Now after all this time, Japanese Ambassador to Russia Masaru Kamizuki recalled The-Holy-One's advice for Japan: "Sign a peace treaty with Russia, even if that meant giving up the Northern Territories. Return Russia to the G8."

I can't believe we're living in a time when Russia is launching its missile into Japan and bombing Hokkaido while I'm over here in Russia, Kamizuki thought. *I can't believe that President Rasputin, a man I've met with many times, is now called a war criminal and treated like Hitler. Russia is my second home, the place I've spent my junior high school days while Father worked for a trading company. At the very least, I won't let this country become an enemy of Japan.* He clenched his lips tightly.

As an ambassador to Russia, Kamizuki made repeated requests to meet with President Rasputin. But Russia was offended by Japan's financial and economic sanctions, along with Japan's supply of bulletproof vests to Ukraine. Moreover, Russia did not expect that the gentle-looking Prime Minister Tabata would expel eight Russian diplomats from Japan, excluding the Russian ambassador to Japan. As expected, the natural gas pipeline project with Russia went out the window, and Japanese people were no longer allowed to visit graves in the Northern Territories without a visa. Negotiations on fisheries and catch limits of fish such as salmon became difficult. Above all, President Rasputin's trust in Japan was completely lost after the Japanese government froze the assets of the president's two daughters. Japan was just following the principle, "If you can't beat 'em, join 'em," but this strategy put the Ambassador to Russia in a difficult position. *It's a shame. More than 80% of Russians used to view Japan favorably*, Kamizuki thought.

Because of the Ukrainian ex-comedian, President Lenlensky, Russia's credibility sank to the lowest of lows. Ukraine turned into a wrestling ring; "Made-in-Russia missiles" were fired into certain parts of Poland and the Czech Republic.

In the first place, France was the only member of the E.U. with nuclear weapons, as the United Kingdom would leave the E.U. And France had only 300 nuclear missiles. On the other hand, Russia still had nearly 7,000 nuclear missiles including 800 submarine-launched ballistic missiles (SLBMs). The E.U. itself can't go to war with Russia unless it becomes a quasi-colony of the United States to be supplied with American nuclear weapons. In fact, America's nuclear weapons had already made their way into the E.U. Japanese news channels reported that going up against NATO forces was Russia's greatest fear, but the real issue was whether to limit the battleground to Ukraine or expand out to the E.U. The sly Obamiden had no intention of turning the United States into a battleground. The same could be said for the U.S.–Japan alliance. The United States was intending to fight against China and North Korea using the lands of South Korea and Japan as its main battleground. U.S. President Obamiden was a coward who only made rallying cries. He was just pulling the strings to see if the people of those countries would continue to worship the United States.

Ambassador Kamizuki brought Japanese-style tatami mats into the Red Square near Moscow's Kremlin. In the background, he set up a golden *byobu* folding screen depicting Mt. Fuji and cherry blossoms. Kamizuki wore a white kimono and built a *seppuku* setup to go on a hunger strike until President Rasputin's anger toward Japan subsided and friendly ties between Japan and

Russia were set in stone. This action in his behalf was clearly distinct from the Ministry of Foreign Affairs of Japan, which was now completely possessed by the late President Obamiden.

8.

Over in Taiwan, the country was enduring the anticipated invasion by China. Gazing over at white smoke and red flashes, President Chu Ingniang thought: *At any cost, we must hold out for a week at least. The United States and Japan should come to help us by then.* The Taiwanese president believed that China would not destroy the entirety of Taiwan, as China was begging for Taiwan's prosperity.

Just then, she received a report detailing that the ICBM launched by North Korea rocketed to a height of 3,700 miles but did not fall to Tokyo, contrary to expectations; instead, it made a 180-degree turn in the direction of North Korea and hit right on the hillside of Mt. Paektu. She further obtained information that the unexpected crash was not an accident but rather the work of some physical force—perhaps Japan's new weapon called "YES, U-turn." Apparently, this ICBM that hit Mt. Paektu was a nuclear missile, and Mt. Paektu suffered a gigantic explosion that sent volcanic bombs to Pyongyang and northeastern China. Subsequent lava flows from the explosion destroyed some nuclear missile facilities. North Korean General Secretary Kim Show-un went missing, but he was thought to have escaped to an underground shelter.

Anyhow, it will be difficult for North Korea and China to launch nuclear missiles into Japan if Japan carried a new counter weapon. There's a higher chance that Japan and the United States will come to help Taiwan, thought Chu Ing-niang.

Another report came in, outlining that the two long-range missiles launched from Taipei into Beijing, China, hit critical areas of the city. According to the report, this attack even caught President Zhen Yuanlai of China by surprise.

Taiwan was left to sporadic missile exchanges

with the Fujian Province across the strait, but it was clear that Fujian was reluctant to follow Beijing's order. They'd been doing business with Taiwan for a long time; they did not want to be hit by Taiwan's missiles and have only southern China suffer a sea of fire. Regarding the military jets in air combat, the F-35s purchased from the United States shot down the enemy with 80% accuracy, and damage to the Taiwan side was kept to around 20%. The U.S. Seventh Fleet would soon arrive. The Japanese Self-Defense Forces and the Australian army would surely come to help. The Taiwanese president also held high expectations for Japan's new weapon.

Meanwhile, the U.S. Seventh Fleet was approaching the Senkaku Islands. Thirty fighter jets with air-to-surface missiles took off from the aircraft carrier *Abraham Lincoln*. China's temporary missile base on the Senkaku Islands was completely demolished and incinerated after their second wave of attack.

The U.S. military launched pinpoint attacks on fake fishing boats from an altitude of 20,000 feet in retaliation for the incident in which the People's Liberation Army, disguising themselves as fishing boats, sank eight JCG vessels with drones. American pilots began attacking the Chinese boats with unmanned aircraft systems or drones from a U.S. base in Arizona as if they were playing a shooting game. From a height of about 20,000 feet, every shot hit the 30-foot boats with precision; Chinese spy ships began to desperately flee after 100 or so ships were shot. Three frigates of the U.S. Navy came in to guard the Senkaku Islands, followed by the arrival of four stealth bombers that had left Guam four hours earlier. Two bombers attacked North Korean troops that were attacking South Korea. They then bombed the remaining North Korean troops in Pyongyang. North Korean anti-aircraft guns couldn't reach the bombers that were flying at an altitude of over 40,000 feet.

The two remaining black-colored, triangular stealth bombers attacked Shanghai and Beijing. The United States had not used nuclear weapons yet; this was a warning.

Japan lagged behind other countries in mobilizing their armed forces, but Prime Minister Tabata finally came out of hiding and gave orders. Japan's Maritime Self-Defense Force and Air Self-Defense Force began to mobilize.

In the United States, Acting President Deborah, a Black woman, gave a brief speech and announced that America would not hesitate to use nuclear weapons to counter any future attacks on South Korea, Japan, and Taiwan. She hinted at the use of ICBM.

The Japanese government also announced that it was ready to use long-range missiles developed by M. Heavy Industries and that they would not hesitate to carry out preemptive attacks on enemy territory, including airports and missile facilities.

It became urgent to pull India into the Quad and to soothe Russia's grudge against the G7, particularly Japan, for the Ukrainian War.

Over at the Ministry of Defense, Agnes watched the war situation with her clairvoyant viewing ability.

Agnes started speaking.

"The South Korean ground force is about to attack North Korea. As for India, The-Holy-One is now persuading Prime Minister Gupta's guardian spirit.

"In Russia, President Rasputin invited Ambassador Kamizuki. The president is telling the ambassador to stop his hunger strike and that he understood Kamizuki's Bushido spirit. He seems to be serving café au lait and cheese-filled flat bread called 'Khachapuri.'

"Well, we need to figure out what to do from this point. Oh, Jesus Christ is trying to send the pope over to Taiwan, too."

Vice-Minister Manobe and Assistant Director Suzumoto listened with a bewildered expression.

9.

Agnes was tired that day, so she decided to head back to the shelter she once stayed at, by the dormitory of Bank of Japan in Daikanyama. Agnes was accompanied by Chief Naoyuki Yamane from the First Criminal Investigation Division and Chief Haruka Kazami from the Public Security Bureau for protection. Yamane and Kazami stayed in the rooms next to Agnes', bringing their teammates in case of any emergency. They made adjustments to receive any communication from the Defense Ministry rather smoothly should the military situation change.

Agnes couldn't sleep until 2 a.m. She then dozed off for two hours.

Was it a dream or reality? She saw Archangel Gabriel descend from heaven and fold in his large wings. This time she got a clear look at Gabriel's facial features. He looked exactly like Chief

Yamane who was sleeping next door—just like Yama-Pi, but blonde. He could probably work for the Secret Service based on his muscular physique.

"Are you Archangel Gabriel?" Agnes asked.

"That's right. You had a rough day yesterday. There is a limit to the miracles we can perform in this world as angels of heaven. The time has come for you to have a stronger sense of mission and to train your mind to a greater extent," Gabriel said.

"What else is left for me to do?"

"You're the only Seraph with a cross-shaped stigma," Gabriel said. "There are four Seraphim, who are the highest-ranked angels that protect our Savior. From now on, Jesus Christ will guide you directly. That means you will be granted a power that far exceeds that of the archbishop of Tokyo and the pope. Transcend worldly status, recognition, and power. Strive to become ever so spiritual."

"I once died, but I was allowed to come back to life. I will dedicate my life to God without escaping into self-preservation."

"That's the mindset. You shall make all sorts of miracles as long as you are with Jesus."

"Um, excuse me for asking, but you look like Chief Yamane who is guarding me."

"I, too, have soul brothers."

"Archangel Gabriel, does that mean Chief Yamane is a portion of your soul on this earth?"

"It will soon be revealed. But you shall not fall in love with him. If you fall in love, you will start to have attachments and make calculations in favor of your worldly interests. That will give the devil a chance to sneak in. Even if he dies, you must fulfill your own mission."

These were harsh words, but Agnes was slightly relieved to know she was not the only angel. She was genuinely glad that she had an ally in this lonesome mission.

Agnes had always loved Jesus. *The miracles in Nagoya couldn't have happened with my own power. They must have happened when Jesus was with me*, she thought.

Jesus must have lent me his powers for the "YES, U-turn" that turned around the trajectory of North Korea's ICBM. North Korea will surely fire several more nuclear missiles at South Korea, Japan, and even mainland America. Nuclear weapons will be ineffective if I'm able to show them that a nuclear missile will make a U-turn every time it is launched. The United States may be able to defend itself with its own military power, but at the very least, I want to protect mainland Japan.

As these thoughts went through her head, Agnes fell back to sleep. After a while, it started getting brighter outside and then morning came.

Agnes headed to the Ministry of Defense for "work."

Okinawa had come under nuclear attack, so first things first, she had to remove the radioactive contamination from the area. *Will I be able to do that with the power of prayer? I'm sure I can.* Agnes prayed to God and to Jesus for about 10 minutes. An enormous tornado appeared in Okinawa, and it moved across the Okinawan sky. TV Asahi, which somehow survived, reported the scene. The tornado sucked in radioactive contaminants like an air purifier and moved in the direction of the Pacific Ocean until it was siphoned into a 6-mile-deep oceanic trench and slowly vanished.

Agnes also learned that the Russian bombers that blasted Sapporo, Hokkaido, had flown out of the now-fortified Northern Territories. She offered a prayer to trigger a great earthquake at the Russian base in the Northern Territories. She prayed for about 10 minutes. Then, a magnitude-8.9 earthquake struck directly below the

Northern Territories. The earth below Russia's air force base began to crack apart, and bombers were sucked in one after another. For some reason, their missile base began to blow up on its own. Khabarovsk, the headquarters of the Eastern Military District of Russia, informed Moscow that an emergency broke out. They flew a jet into the sky, saw black smoke rising all over the Northern Territories, and learned that their base was almost entirely destroyed. The Russians suspected that Japan used a cutting-edge tectonic weapon, as the Russians, too, were researching tectonic weapons. There was a large fault in the west coast of the United States, so the Russians were thinking of using satellites to attack the fault and create a large, artificial earthquake if possible.

Russia was frustrated that Japan was ahead of them. In the eyes of the Eastern Military District, Joint Strategic Command in Khabarovsk, Japan's satellites supposedly attacked the Northern Territories with some kind of electromagnetic waves to trigger a man-made earthquake. The Russians had yet to know that God had answered the power of Agnes' prayer. Soon after that, five ICBMs were launched from Alaska and fell onto major Russian cities.

Russian President Rasputin was taken aback by the report handed over by his secretary.

Ambassador Kamizuki, who was in meditation, opened his eyes widely. He turned to Rasputin and made a strong proposal: "Now is the time for you to declare friendship with Japan." It was as if Kamizuki was overtaken by God. Even Rasputin, an eighth-degree black belt holder in judo, shivered.

"I'll reconsider it," Rasputin said. "Your God, and Russia's God, must be the same being."

It was a step forward.

10.

The following day was tragic for the Ministry of Defense. Two drones flew over from a park nearby and suddenly attacked the ministry's building.

The seventh floor where Agnes stayed was fine, but the windows shattered and fell to the ground after the building was attacked from the southern and northern directions.

The drones appeared to have been a modified version. After launching a small missile, the drones themselves became bombs and exploded inside the ministry. The perpetrator must have intended to leave no evidence. The terrorists were likely remote-controlling the drones from a room in a nearby hotel.

Agnes ran down the emergency stairs from a special room on the seventh floor. On the third-floor landing, she met Chief Yamane and Chief Kazami, who came running up the stairs.

"Oh! Ms. Suzu Nomura, you're safe," Yamane said.

It was then that Agnes realized she went by the name of "Suzu Nomura" within the ministry when other people were around.

To be honest, she wanted to talk about Archangel Gabriel with Yamane and dive into his arms. But Yamane was always faithful to his duties. Haruka Kazami was also worried about Agnes and asked if she was injured. Someone else came down from an upper floor and shouted that Parliamentary Secretary Kanayama was in critical condition. Alas, even the Ministry of Defense was no longer safe.

Even Agnes had overlooked the drone attack while she was indoors, talking to someone. Chief Yamane thought that spies in the ministry leaked information about Agnes to the terrorists, so the drone attack was aimed specifically at her. The enemy was coming closer and closer to the truth.

People in the ministry knew very well that Japan did not have a new weapon. Thus, Agnes, who had suddenly started visiting the ministry, was suspected to be a psychic.

It was unlikely that Vice-Minister Manobe and Assistant Director Kazumi Suzumoto of the Ministry of Defense had leaked details, but news about the "YES, U-turn" made against North Korea's ICBM, and the tornado that eliminated radioactive contamination in Okinawa, were certainly reported to Defense Minister Takasugi through some channel. Takasugi should've reported to the prime minister, so there must've been an interception or wiretapping during that exchange. Alas, it had become difficult to remotely operate Japan's national defense from within the Ministry of Defense. Many lives in the ministry would be lost. There were crowds of fire trucks, ambulances, and police cars roaming around outside.

Chief Yamane and his colleague planned on taking Agnes as far away as possible, where they would catch a cab and secretively transport her to another hiding place.

While the three of them were running along the moat, however, they were suddenly targeted by a sniper who was scoping them out from the roof of a building. The bullet barely missed, dropping a willow leaf and greatly rippling the water in the moat.

"They have a psychic on their side, too. They know about my powers," Agnes said.

"I'm an ex-Secret Service agent. I'm used to protecting VIPs. I'll form a team of five that can work like the Secret Service within an hour, so for now, let's run to that department store," Yamane said.

The opponent used a rifle so it would be difficult for them to target Agnes among a crowd of people. But if there were multiple terrorists, they would be able to communicate with each other and coordinate an attack on Agnes with a pistol or a knife. That would be a problem.

Yamane and Haruka Kazami sandwiched Agnes from front and back, and the three of them fled into a café inside the nearby department store. Yamane asked the Metropolitan Police Department to send in Secret Service agents as support.

"It's all right," Agnes told Yamane. "Now that I know I'm being targeted, I'm not afraid of bullets and knives. I just need to keep my guard up. But if the opponent is a mind reader with a clairvoyant viewing ability, they'll be able to identify our location by reading our minds. So instead of thinking about our real selves, imagine that Ms. Kazami and I are office workers in Marunouchi district. And Mr. Yamane, think of yourself as a banker. Think about Hibiya Park from time to time, and do not think about the incident in the ministry."

Yamane, after being told that he was a banker, thought of the hidden, underground vault of the Bank of Japan. He thought that the vault would withstand bombs and even prevent the psychic's telepathy.

"No, Mr. Yamane," Agnes said. "We can't live next to bundles of cash in the Bank of Japan's underground vault."

Oh my goodness. Agnes has already read my mind. Yamane felt it difficult to empty out his thoughts.

After a while, old Secret Service friends of Yamane arrived. Instead of communicating with them verbally, Yamane wrote a memo in his notebook.

Help us get to a safe place. This girl is a living national treasure. I'll explain later.

The three officers once worked for Yamane. They were Kazuo Minegishi, Susumu Takarada, and Chiemi Anzai. *There're five of us, including*

Public Security's Haruka Kazami and myself. That will give us a basic formation to guard a VIP, Yamane thought.

"Um, Ms. Haruka Kazami," Yamane said. "You're an office worker, and you graduated from the University of Tokyo, right? Is studying your specialty?"

"Sorry to disappoint you, but I'm a third-degree in aikido. Well, I was often targeted by molesters and stalkers, so I only became defiant. As for studying, I'm as good as an ordinary University of Tokyo student. After all, I was recruited for my physical stamina," Kazami answered.

"So you can deal with one-on-one fights, huh?" Minegishi said.

"I also did Japanese archery, so my eyesight is very good. I'd like to be a sniper someday," Kazami said.

The waitress brought coffee and tea.

Chiemi Anzai said, "Oh! They serve wonderful chocolate parfait here." Of course, she, too, pretended to be an office worker. She wore plain clothes so there should be no problem.

Susumu Takarada followed suit in pretending to make small talk. He said to Yamane, "I've always thought you would be good as an actor. I hope you can switch careers one day and play a role in a crime show or something."

"Come to think of it," Yamane said, "you look like an actress named something-Ayase, Ms. Haruka Kazami."

"Yep, the only thing we have in common is that we both come from a farm in Okayama."

As the five of them acted out these conversations, they communicated by writing out their next step. They decided to use the now-empty court dormitory in Ikedayama as a temporary shelter for the Metropolitan Police Department.

"I heard that masked palm civets appear there," Yamane said.

With that, they left the café and took the subway train. They headed toward Shinagawa Ward, praying that the terrorists did not have an organized faction.

11.

Empress Emerita Michiko grew up here, in Ikedayama. The area was safe, with a high level of
prestige, and it was easy to spot any suspicious
strangers walking around. There were two police
boxes in this area, so Yamane and the others were
able to count on extra assistance if an emergency
broke out. In the corner of a row of mansions,
there was a plot of land sized about 1,200 sq.
yd.; on this land stood a rather old building con-
structed of reinforced concrete, large enough to
house at least nine families. This building used to
be a dormitory for the Supreme Court of Japan.
Several years ago, when actress Tomoko Matsuy-
ama graduated from an idol group named AKB
and starred in her first movie called *The Cursed
Complex*, it was rumored that the movie was
filmed there. There was a little bamboo grove
nearby, and many neighbors reported that they

saw masked palm civets.

"It might smell a little moldy in here, but this place isn't noticeable," Yamane said. "There's also a convenience store close by so we can easily get food. Ms. Suzu, do you know the difference between the Self-Defense Forces and the police?"

"The Self-Defense Forces have a cooking vehicle and camp tents. The police don't."

"Bingo! We cops buy *bento*, or pre-made meals, and get canned coffee from the vending machine. So actually, we're not very good at lodging security," Yamane said.

"You think of us two girls as housekeepers or somethin'?" Kazami grumbled.

"Actually, I've cooked poisoned curry before. I wanted to find out the lethal dose for humans. Besides, I'm good at pushing men around and making them clean," Anzai said.

"There, there, calm down," Minegishi chimed in. "We'll take turns buying food, and I'll call over some available members from the Identification Section to clean the apartment."

They set up a lodge using rooms for four families on the third floor. They installed surveillance cameras near the entrances, exits, and corridors, along with infrared lights that would emit a *ding dong* sound whenever someone entered or exited at night. They prayed that no raccoon-dog-like civets would appear. They also set up another surveillance camera on the roof for extra precaution and prepared machine guns in the rooms of Chief Yamane and Sergeant Minegishi in case of an organized terrorist attack. As a side note, the chief was superior to the sergeant as an inspector.

That night seemed to pass by without any incidents. In her dream, Agnes, a.k.a. Suzu Nomura, was reviewing the world of saviors of the ninth dimension that she once visited. This time, she could see the face of Lord God El Cantare quite distinctly. The Lord God was sitting on a throne in a room made of diamonds. A series of screens appeared before the throne, one after another, and the Lord was observing the events on Earth. One screen showed Agnes and the others at Ikeday-ama. Another screen replayed a scene of "YES, U-turn" that was performed on North Korea's nuclear missile, while a different screen played a scene of the tornado in Okinawa.

The Lord knows everything, Agnes thought.

Another scene showed how part of the Lord Himself was incarnated into a man, who was praying and conducting remote viewing inside the Temple of Messiah in Tokyo. *Oh, the Lord is constantly watching over our entire world*, thought Agnes, and before she knew it, tears streamed down her face. Just then, the one on the screen looked back at Agnes. He could see her from across the screen. It was the man that everyone referred to as "The-Holy-One."

Agnes glued her eyes to the screen. The-Holy-

One was calling over to god Zulu in Africa. This must have been a scene from one or two years ago. God Zulu had a bull-like face with horns. He looked capable of fighting even the devil with the silver-tipped spear he carried in his right hand. He was well over 10 feet tall, maybe around 17 feet or so.

The-Holy-One—yes, a part of the Lord God—seemed to be questioning god Zulu about China's sin for spreading the coronavirus. God Zulu responded, "I shall bring them a bad harvest," and he generated hundreds of billions of locusts from central and eastern parts of Africa. The swarm of locusts became like a cloud and moved east by riding the prevailing westerlies. The Chinese government learned of the locusts, and they deployed 100,000 ducks to the neighboring Pakistan to intercept the desert locusts that would fly down to the fields and feast on grains. At least, that was their plan.

The swarm of desert locusts could not be stopped in Pakistan. They finally flew into mainland China and attacked crops such as rice and wheat. The fields were stripped empty and bare in no time.

Oh, God governs bad harvests and famine, too. Agnes understood that God uses the power of Mother Nature to express His Divine Will of opposition against oppressive regimes and human rights abuses. *That must have been the case with the flooding of the Yangtze and Yellow Rivers in China that are shown on other screens*, she thought. *It was unheard of for tens of millions of houses to be swept away by flooding. However, the Chinese government censored information so that scenes of houses being swept away were not shown on TV; only the photos taken by civilians on smartphones circulated among some people on the Internet. Will the people of China realize that they are being held responsible for the sup-*

*pression of human rights in the Uyghur Autono-
mous Region and for the artificial production of
the coronavirus? Will people realize God's Will
or the Divine Will? Or will they continue to live
as servants of President Zhen Yuanlai?*

*China calls itself a democracy, but the coun-
try has no idea what the sovereignty of the people
entails. They arouse fear in the people of China
by oppressing them. Just as Chairman Mao Zedong invaded Southern Mongolia, the Uyghur
Region, and Tibet, President Zhen Yuanlai
believes he can only become a true autocrat by
absorbing Taiwan. Today, China thinks they don't
need a real God. They intend to make the First
Emperor of Qin, Qin Shi Huang, along with Mao
Zedong and Zhen Yuanlai, into a divine lineage
of God. Just as Tibet has a government-in-exile,
China believes Taiwan should also establish a
government-in-exile in Malaysia or elsewhere.
China plans on ousting Taiwanese President Chu*

Ing-niang with a single blow, but the Taiwan issue is not an internal affair as China claims it to be. Taiwan, a country with freedom, democracy, faith, and a parliamentary system, gained its independence from Japan. It was never once ruled by the People's Republic of China. At least The-Holy-One is thinking as such, and he is trying to defend Taiwan.

Agnes fell into a deep sleep as she thought about what she could do.

12.

Mt. Aso erupted. The volcanic flame reached up to 10,000 feet above the crater and sent volcanic bombs and ashfall over the entire Kyushu region. Pyroclastic flows occurred as well. The eruption was not of the same kind as that of Mt. Paektu in North Korea.

Yet she had a bad feeling. Agnes, a.k.a. Suzu Nomura, sensed that Japan was in imminent danger. Since the major newspaper companies in Japan had lost their head offices, they published newspapers that were eight or so pages in length with the cooperation of local newspaper companies. For some reason, among the TV stations, only TV Asahi in Roppongi was still operating. Rumor had it that TV Asahi was kept intact because the enemy countries highly evaluated its lenient attitude when reporting about North Korea, China, and Russia; they also wanted to get the latest information about Japan via broadcast.

One day, around 4 p.m., news broke out that the *Bungeishunjusha*, a publishing company in Kioicho, was blown up and that another publishing company, *Shinchosha*, was almost simultaneously destroyed. At first, these attacks were thought to be done by drones, similar to the recent drone attack on the Ministry of Defense. The Metropolitan Police Department's Counterterrorism Unit announced that based on various analyses, the attacks on the two publishing companies were carried out by the Chinese, as with the previous drone attack. In response, the Beijing spokesperson made an angry comment: "Japan's announcement is completely outrageous, and it has deeply hurt the peace-loving civilians of China. We firmly demand an apology from the Japanese government." Chief Yamane said, "Look who's speaking. What peace-loving civilians of China? China probably kept TV Asahi because they wanted to keep broadcasting this kind of news."

It was strange that only the buildings of *Bungeishunjusha* and *Shinchosha* were completely destroyed, whereas no damage was done to the surrounding buildings. There was a high chance that it was a drone attack: launching missiles from high above the buildings. It was the kind of attack only the U.S. military could execute: launching a highly accurate attack from an altitude of 20,000 feet and striking a target that is as small as 30 feet without being noticed by Japan's Self-Defense Forces. Weekly magazines such as the *Shukan Bunshun* and *Shukan Shincho* played a role in forming the public opinion among Japanese citizens after the major newspapers lost their influence; nevertheless, circulating photos of the former magazine's editor-in-chief's neck, torso, and limbs blown away, along with photos of the burned corpse of the latter magazine's editor-in-chief strongly suggested the attacks on the two publishing companies to be some sort of retaliation.

After all, these magazines had kept calling President Rasputin insane, a mass murderer, and the Second Hitler every week in the midst of the Ukrainian War.

Still, it was rather eye-opening that both publishing companies were taken down in flames and more than two-thirds of their employees were either killed or injured. Times had changed, indeed. Even though weekly magazines were unreliable, news on the Internet was too noisy and messy to read.

Just then, Yamane received a phone call from Nakayama, director of the First Criminal Investigation Division at the headquarters.

According to Nakayama's phone call, an analysis of the U.S. military showed that low-altitude missiles of about 700 feet were launched from a North Korean submarine that had secretly entered the Tokyo Bay. Apparently, the missiles flew as they dodged a cluster of buildings and hit the two publishing companies. Given the terrifying accuracy of the missiles, Nakayama said no announcement would be made for the time being so as not to frighten Japanese citizens. He added that four anti-submarine helicopters from Japan were chasing down the North Korean target, and the Japanese government would make an announcement as soon as they destroyed the enemy submarine.

Yamane sighed.

"We're screwed. Chinese drones attacked the Ministry of Defense. Sixty percent of the world's drones are made in China, so I think their technology is advanced, and the guys who attacked us the other day must be Chinese terrorists and psychics. Today's attacks on the publishing companies might've been pinpoint attacks by highly accurate missiles from North Korea. Our ministers will definitely go into hiding again. It's getting out of hand even for the cops, especially since at least two-and-a-half million Chinese people live in Japan."

"Mr. Yamane, there's something more important I need to tell you," Agnes said. "I can't help but feel that Japan itself is in danger. There are too many earthquakes on the Pacific Coast of the Japanese archipelago, especially around Tokyo. What if Mt. Fuji erupts? Now that Mt. Aso erupted, it's becoming an increasingly real possibility. I'm also scared of an earthquake directly below Tokyo, or a huge tsunami. It would be beyond my power to avert these."

"What makes you think that's gonna happen?" Yamane asked.

"It's God. Sure, there are many bad countries abroad, but I can't say that Japan is a good one either. Materialism and atheism have spread so much here that we're no different from China. I mean, even with Mr. Obamiden's democracy, in the end, it is 'democracy without God.' To me, it's an existentialist view of life. They're just telling us to protect our earthly lives and that it's good enough if we feel happiness only while we're alive. Back when President Donald King was in office, he said, 'Open the church doors even when the coronavirus is spreading. Don't reject the people seeking salvation from God.' Mr. Obamiden only talked about competing for worldly prosperity and advocating for equality of human rights, all without faith. Russia's President Rasputin has religious faith but people called him the devil. There's something wrong."

Yamane, too, was beginning to sense something ever since he came into contact with Agnes. He was starting to think that things like God and faith exist above a body of nation ruled by law.

After a day filled with bad news, Agnes was almost certain she would have a nightmare.

Sure enough, "it" came around 2:30 a.m. Agnes did not panic because she quickly recognized it was the devil.

The devil spoke. "I am the one who tempted Jesus. Jesus was a helpless man who couldn't turn stone into bread, who couldn't perform any miracles even after I told him to jump off a cliff, as the angels would spread their wings and save him. After all, he was sold for a small amount of money by one of his twelve disciples, and he was nailed to the cross. If the God he believed in was real, why didn't He save Jesus?"

"No," Agnes refuted. "After I was shot dead, the Lord God welcomed me to His throne in heaven. He allowed my resurrection. During the time of Jesus, too, his resurrection after the crucifixion went on to become the core of Christian faith. Humans *experience*, but God *creates*. Your argument is powerless."

"Devils have an eternal life, but you humans

have only finite lives," the devil said. "God can't even win against manmade weapons such as drones or missiles. And now, we devils are ruling this earth. Even if one or two angels come down on earth, they are of no use. Can you stop nuclear missiles from Russia, China, and North Korea? Can you stop the United States' nuclear missiles (ICBM) from mass murdering people in opposing countries? Can you stop the division of the United Nations?"

"You must be Beelzebub, the second strongest in hell. You're only rebellious because you're always jealous of God. You manipulate sleepiness and lust, but the devil can't rule a stainless soul."

"It's easy to delude a sister like yourself," Beelzebub said. "How did you feel when you were being raped by four young boys? Did it make you happy? Did you enjoy killing the four strong men who attacked you? You're getting old enough to feel the pleasure of being loved by a real man.

Like Mary Magdalene, you need to have sex with as many men as you can and become a master of sex; only then will you become the bride of Jesus."

"I was once dead. My soul resurrected, so my mission is to teach people about the spiritual life and the real world that was created by God. It's no use tempting me. I'm already the bride of Jesus, and I'm the daughter of Heavenly Father. I, too, would rather die on the cross than give in to your temptations. What's wrong with a woman with the cross dying on the cross?"

The devil sighed deeply and continued.

"You should know this. A war is always set up by the devil. I wonder if you can stand one billion, or two billion, people dying one after another. Through the 'Coronavirus War,' we've already created nearly one billion infected people and killed tens of millions. Most of them will curse God and become soldiers of hell."

"My faith will not waver. I will save the souls of the dead, and I will save the souls of the living. A missile may kill the human flesh, but it cannot kill the sacred soul. When humankind is living in an age of crises, we are also living in an age of God's miracle. The Lord, Jesus Christ, and Agnes here are one."

"Good grief. You would be happier by marrying Yamane, having a family with him, and raising children together. It's a shame. How ignorant, how arrogant, and how foolish you are to go up against the entire legion of devils. Let me bestow you with the torments of hell once more…"

Just then, Archangel Michael came to the rescue. "Agnes, you're not alone." He then drove Beelzebub away.

13.

Setting aside Japanese Ambassador to Russia Kamizuki's *kamikaze*-attack-like move, the Russian government was angry at President Lenlensky's trickster-like maneuver of Ukrainian defense. They thought that Ukraine was pressing their luck too much by receiving military support from NATO. Upon receiving a report that Moskva, a guided missile cruiser and the flagship of Russia's Black Sea Fleet, was attacked and sunk by Ukrainian cruise missiles, President Rasputin made a critical decision.

1. Ukrainian President Lenlensky must be captured or sent to hell.

2. Russia will destroy the capital city of Kiev (Kyiv).

3. Russia will not hesitate to use nuclear weapons on any country that supports Ukraine or plans on joining NATO.

4. Russia will ultimately corner NATO and pressure it into dissolving.

President Rasputin couldn't hold back his anger. Everywhere around the globe, the media was full of fake news. There were only 175,000 Russian troops surrounding 200,000 Ukrainian troops from the north, east, and south. Had Russia not made a military intervention at this time, the Ukrainian army would've committed genocide against the people of Crimea and the two independent regions with many ethnic Russians in eastern Ukraine—falling into the plot of U.S. President Obamiden. *I will never allow Ukraine to trick the E.U. and NATO into setting Russia up to be the world's enemy, turning President Lenlensky into a "hero" and me into "the second coming of Hitler."* As a worst-case scenario, President Rasputin was determined to fire 6,000 nuclear missiles at troublesome E.U. countries and at the United States of America. *Even God will not allow America's self-righteous leadership to continue*, he thought.

In fact, even the Russian Orthodoxy, which had supported President Rasputin, and the Vatican's pope came to be at odds. A religious war was another underlying factor. Fifty percent of American youth and children were either materialists or did not believe in any religion, and there was even a new movement to protect this younger generation against bullying.

Everything was brought upon by Obamiden's spiritual disposition to attract low-grade spirits.

That night, President Rasputin was alone in his prayer room. He meditated for about 30 minutes, asking God if he held any wrong thoughts and if his thoughts were driven by selfish desires. A sphere of light descended from heaven. A moment later, a one-eyed, elderly man with a cane appeared out of the light.

"You must be God Odin," addressed Rasputin.

"It is an honor that you have been protecting this northern country for 10,000 years. In the past, Russia, the three Baltic countries, Germany, Britain, and Ukraine, who we are now at war with, all revered you as king. Now, America is taking the lead to bring Ukraine into NATO to isolate Russia and expel this country from the international community. If it was my ego that brought this about, please discipline and correct me. But if my desire to protect and to restore Russia is in accordance with God's Will, please guide me in the right direction."

Odin spoke.

"Rasputin, it is I, who is trying to save Russia from atheism and materialism and to guide this country toward new prosperity. Western countries, on the other hand, consider your long-term regime as the reflection of a dictator's ego. I, myself, am a part of Lord God El Cantare. America, too, under men such as George Washington and

Lincoln, was once guided by God Thoth, who is also a part of El Cantare. President Donald King listened to the voice of God Thoth. That is why you two could understand each other. On the contrary, Obamiden and Vice President Deborah, who is now the acting president, cannot hear the voice of God Thoth. Thus, they misunderstand you as the devil. They are stuck to the belief that they can be in power by gaining popularity via the media, which is just a gathering of ordinary people. The former comedian and current president of Ukraine, Lenlensky, is acting as a hero, when in fact, he is just a poster child of this TV era.

"In other words, both Obamiden and Lenlensky mistakenly think of the media's collective thoughts as 'God.' God Thoth is deeply concerned. God Ame-no-Mioya-Gami of Japan, also a part of El Cantare, is ashamed that Japan is losing faith in God and turning into a country of materialism and worldly benefits. Establish good relations with Japan and with India, which is guided by Shakyamuni Buddha, another branch spirit of El Cantare. Now, here, God's Will is to guide the United States to real faith and to introduce freedom, democracy, faith, and a parliamentary system into the atheist country of China.

"Hold strong faith and pressure Lenlensky to leave the political arena. The Ukrainian people are your brothers and sisters. Open a path so that together, Russia and Ukraine can create a brighter future."

President Rasputin was relieved to gain assurance that it was God's wish to protect Russia. Moreover, God alluded to the death of U.S. President Obamiden. *So he was dead after all*, he thought. But according to CNN, Obamiden fell while playing golf owing to a mild stroke, and he would be hospitalized for about a month. Rasputin told himself: *I will somehow find a way to fight it out with Acting President Deborah until President Donald King is elected as the next U.S. President. Also, I'll pave the way for friendly relations with Japan and India.*

Rasputin decided to tell Ambassador Kamizuki that Russia would be willing to return the four northern islands, no longer usable for military purposes, to Japan under the conditions that Japanese Prime Minister Tabata would not blindly follow the United States; that he wishes for former Prime Minister Ando, or someone else who can follow in his footsteps, to become the next prime minister; and that these efforts will lead to a peace treaty between Russia and Japan. *As long as Russia and Japan believe in the same God, the two countries should be able to join hands with each other*, Rasputin thought. He decided to wait for the former U.S. president to return to his role while fostering cooperative relations with India.

China waged the Coronavirus War on the world, and now, the virus is starting to spread in their own country. The number of infections in China will rise to millions, tens of millions, and hundreds of millions. As the law goes, "You reap what you sow."

Rasputin processed his thoughts up to this point. The-Holy-One in Tokyo had already read through his thought process, and he communicated Rasputin's change of mind to Agnes as a vision in her mind.

Agnes braced herself. *I have at last entered the realm of God. Soon, the day will come when I must fulfill my mission as one of the Seraphim.*

That mission was to purify Japan and to bring peace to the war-torn world—the calling of a new age that no past savior was able to accomplish.

14.

Here in Ginza, Agnes was eating *unaju*, a dish of eel over rice, at a restaurant called Chikuyotei. Vice-Minister Manobe of the Ministry of Defense said he wanted to see her for the first time in a while, so the meal was his treat.

Manobe spoke to Agnes. "Ever since the eruption of Mt. Paektu, North Korea has been losing power, and now, Japan, America, and South Korea are gaining the upper hand. We are working hard to destroy the remaining missile sites in North Korea and capture Kim Show-un. North Korea has about 550 operational aircraft and 74 MiG fighter jets, and only 20% of them are functioning, which means we now have air superiority. Our Maritime Self-Defense Force attacked North Korea's 25 submarines with anti-submarine helicopters, destroyers, and submarines, so their submarines are almost completely destroyed. My question to you is, which underground shelter is protecting Kim Show-un?"

Manobe then laid out a map of the Korean Peninsula before Agnes. Agnes was chewing on eel, so despite bad etiquette, she used her chopsticks and pointed to a city on the map called Nampo in North Korea.

Manobe just said, "Okay," and made a phone call. Fifteen minutes later, a bomber took off from the U.S. Seventh Fleet and fired dozens of "bunker buster" bombs on the location Agnes had pointed to. The elevator leading down to the underground shelter went up in flames and the transfer tunnels from the shelter were crushed. Kim Show-un died at age 40-something. Kim Yo-jow, his sister and North Korea's second-in-command, who was hiding in a farmhouse on the outskirts of Pyongyang, was captured by the South Korean military. Now, the Kim dynasty collapsed, and the remaining missile sites were destroyed one by one. A double of Kim Show-un shouted, "Do or Die!" in a fake TV news broadcast, but he was shot in an internal revolt. He was apparently the last double. Thus, it was decided that North Korea would be placed under U.N. control and annexed to South Korea after their nuclear weapons were dismantled.

The country that was most surprised upon hearing this news was the People's Republic of China, which was at war with Taiwan. If China was like the teeth, North Korea, albeit small, was like the lips that protected them. The collapse of North Korea had a significant impact.

Chinese President Zhen Yuanlai was disappointed. *Even with its nuclear weapons, North Korea couldn't defend itself, huh.*

On the other hand, President Chu Ing-niang of Taiwan was delighted. She expected that the United States and Japanese forces would soon come to their rescue. There was also an independence movement in southern China, and if attacked by both the United States and Japan, the southern region would surely fall. In fact, Taiwan's bombardment and missile attacks alone sank 50 landing ships of China's Navy, and Chinese tanks sank along with the ships. The Taiwanese president believed China was unlikely to launch a nuclear attack on Taiwan because if they used nuclear weapons, it would go against China's long-argued logic that the Taiwan issue was an internal affair.

Things didn't go so smoothly, though. The U.S. Seventh Fleet's aircraft carrier *Abraham Lincoln* was suddenly attacked by a hypersonic ICBM launched from China's inland province of Sichuan. America's radars couldn't detect the missile because it was flying while meandering at a very low altitude, about 160 feet above sea level. The missile then floated above just before the aircraft carrier and penetrated its deck. The rumor was real. China had a new weapon.

The U.S. military was stunned by the fact that its aircraft carrier *Lincoln* burst into flames and exploded with one blow by China.

The Lincoln was sunk by a single missile.

The Japanese Maritime Self-Defense Force, Royal Australian Navy, Indian Navy, Royal Navy of the United Kingdom, and the French Navy were equally shocked by the news.

The Acting U.S. President Deborah was furious upon hearing that their aircraft carrier sank. Deborah ordered four nuclear-armed ICBMs to be fired from Guam. She wanted to demolish China's missile site in Sichuan Province. Ironically, and unfortunately, the Guam-launched ICBMs fell on the Uyghurs in the Uyghur Autonomous Region and on the Tibetans in the Tibetan Autonomous Region. One of them also fell on over 1,000 pandas that lived across Tibet and Sichuan Province. The entirety of the mountains, including the bamboo grove, went up in flames, and

500 pandas were killed. China's foreign ministry spokesperson upsettingly criticized the United States, warning: "China will surely avenge the deaths of these pandas, our diplomats for peace."

Surprisingly, China launched, from their satellites, four nuclear attacks targeting New York City, Washington D.C., Houston, and Los Angeles. Acting President Deborah, with her short political career, had no idea that nuclear missiles could fall from right above her head.

The Chinese foreign ministry spokesperson made an announcement: "Eighty years ago, the United States of America dropped two atomic bombs on Hiroshima and Nagasaki and committed genocide. They must pay for their crime."

Deborah had no response. She lacked the knowledge that the U.S. military had dropped the atomic bombs on Japan to protect China.

The U.S. military grew increasingly distrustful of Acting President Deborah. Then, without reading the room, U.S. Press Secretary Pzaki announced the death of President Obamiden, followed by the breaking news that Vice President Deborah would become president.

In the United States, rumors spread that the CIA was plotting to assassinate President Deborah, as if they were true. The world was rapidly losing leaders.

Meanwhile, Russia abruptly dropped a special bomb on Kiev (Kyiv), where Ukrainian President Lenlensky was sound asleep. CNN and BBC aired emergency reports.

The special bomb, which sucks in oxygen within a 0.3-mile radius, was dropped on Kiev while President Lenlensky was asleep. As if drifting off into eternal sleep, Ukrainian leaders and even the animals died off.

Ukraine's "clown" died peacefully in his sleep, just like Snow White.

15.

When Chinese satellites nuked New York, Washington D.C., Houston, and Los Angeles, the new U.S. President Deborah was trembling in an underground bunker of the White House. The TV screen in front of her showed ruins far worse than Hiroshima or Nagasaki during World War II.

"So this is the gift I get for my presidential inauguration?"

Katherine Deborah, the first Black woman to serve as president, was seized with anger that grew far stronger than her fear.

She ordered Paneller, chairperson of the Joint Chiefs of Staff, to deploy Operation "No Tomorrow for China." It was an all-out attack by the U.S. military.

In Japan, Vice-Minister Manobe had just told Agnes about the sinking of the U.S. aircraft carrier *Lincoln* and the nuclear attack from Chinese satellites on the United States. He was asking her about future predictions based on her supernatural powers, along with her opinions about what action Japan should take. They had moved from the collapsed building of the Ministry of Defense and established a branch office within the Ministry of Foreign Affairs.

Agnes said that the clash of political and military powers between the United States and China would only invite a tragic future. She also mentioned that a divine punishment would soon befall humanity lacking any faith in God.

Then, torrential rain began to pour all over China.

The Yangtze and Yellow Rivers rose like an ocean, and a huge whirlpool began to form in Dongting Lake.

The other day, Agnes had spoken with god Zulu in Africa and learned about a goddess named Dongting Lake Niangniang, who had fought against the First Qin Emperor in the past. According to god Zulu, the goddess had a similar kind of anger toward the current President Zhen Yuanlai, and she was supporting the democracy movement in Taiwan and southern China.

"Something terrible will happen there," Agnes said.

Several huge typhoons were formed, and they swept away tens of millions of houses throughout China. Next, not missiles but powerful fireballs fell over Beijing and other major Chinese cities.

China's gigantic trophy buildings turned into beehives as if they had been showered by tens of thousands of missiles. Not only that, Chinese bullet trains, which acted as the main artery of their nation, were blown off the elevated tracks; at airports, passenger planes and military planes alike were torn apart as if they were toys and sent flying in the air; a convoy of cars that fled down the road were rolled up into the sky and thrown into the Pacific Ocean.

How could that beautiful and gentle goddess have exerted such tremendous power? Chinese warships were flipped over by the surging waves, and even the submarines crashed into rocks on the seabed and sank. It was an unprecedented catastrophe in Chinese history.

The exact damage dealt was still unknown, but it was estimated that half of the 1.4 billion Chinese population died within the span of two or three days. Chairperson Paneller of the Joint Chiefs of Staff asked Secretary of Defense Maxwell if Operation "No Tomorrow for China" was still necessary. The United States suffered several million casualties; on the other end, China's population was cut in half.

President Deborah asked the secretary of defense what they should do with Russia. "Ukraine understood that the war won't end as long as they continue to seek help from NATO, so it seems that Ukraine decided to become one of Russia's satellite states and pledge neutrality," he said.

"Rasputin's dictatorship destroyed the world order in the first place," said President Deborah. "Dictatorship must be eliminated from this world and political leaders must be replaced by democratic presidents like me. We must get rid of all dictators who are acting like Hitler. President Lenlensky of Ukraine gave so many speeches on satellite TV. We need to frame him into a hero who fought against a Hitler- or Napoleon-like guy."

Thus, Operation "No Tomorrow for China" was transitioned into Operation "No Tomorrow for Russia."

The operation was narrowed down to three goals:

1. Assassinate President Rasputin.

2. Reduce Russia's economic power to the extent that they cannot remain in the G20.

3. Demilitarize Russia so that the Russian military can never again invade another country, just as America imposed Article 9 on the Japanese Constitution.

Both Secretary of State Pumpkin and Defense Minister Maxwell suggested letting the E.U. negotiate with Russia, as there would be severe damage to the United States, too. They believed that an exchange of nuclear missile attacks between the United States and Russia would most likely be a battle with no winner.

Secretary of State Pumpkin also explained that President Obamiden's basic strategy was for the United States and Russia to fight a proxy war, with Japan as its main battleground, so that he could make an excuse and say that the United States was not defeated by Russia or China— even if Japan was completely beaten down, like Ukraine. "Such a policy is necessary to secure the victory of the next presidential election," Pumpkin added.

However, the first female Black president wanted to have her name recorded in the history books. Deborah decided to directly command Chairperson Paneller; she was adamant about removing Rasputin and destroying Russia's nuclear forces.

The attack on Moscow began from Poland. ICBMs were launched from Guam, Hawaii, Alaska, and the U.S. mainland. Then, U-2 nuclear bombers took off from America's west coast and Guam.

This surprised Rasputin. *Is the new U.S. president an amateur? Three hundred ICBMs were launched out of the blue from the U.S. mainland. We can't intercept them all, but we must completely beat down the White House and the Pentagon*, he thought. From the Central Military District in Russia, Rasputin fired about 10 hypersonic missiles that would circle the globe at a speed of Mach 20 to turn the White House and the Pentagon into ashes. He intended on protecting Moscow like a hedgehog by surrounding the area with interceptor missiles. Rasputin then moved into a nuclear shelter command center that was half a mile underground.

Nevertheless, all 300 U.S. ICBMs exploded midair, either over the Pacific or the Atlantic Ocean. The U-2 bombers became inoperable owing to instrument failure.

The globe-encircling missiles flying at a speed of Mach 20 were blown midair by someone, or something, that moved faster than the missiles. *Maybe it was done by The-Holy-One*, Agnes thought.

16.

U.S. President Katherine Deborah could no longer contain her anger.

"Three hundred ICBMs were shot down? And the U-2 bombers all had instrument failure so they couldn't attack? Impossible. There's just no way. Whoever it is, I won't forgive them. Even if it was God," Deborah said.

Hesitantly, Secretary of Defense Maxwell reported to her.

"It seems like Russia's hypersonic nuclear missiles also vanished without a trace."

"Russia's ICBMs are antiques. They just couldn't reach us," Deborah said. "There might be enemy spies in the U.S. Air Force, or some country might have developed a secret weapon. Get me the best psychic in the United States so we can figure out what's going on."

Having realized there was no point in arguing with her, the defense secretary ordered CIA Director Glinton to find the best psychic in the nation.

The names of candidates were delivered within 10 minutes.

"Cassandra Dixon, age 35. The granddaughter of Ms. Jeane Dixon, the woman who predicted President Kennedy's assassination. Apparently, she's the best psychic we've got now," the defense secretary told Deborah.

"Bring her in, now. I'll give you one hour." It was an executive order.

Thus, America's no. 1 psychic, Ms. Cassandra Dixon, was invited by the head of the White House.

"The United States fired 300 ICBMs at Russia and all 300 missiles suddenly disappeared from our radar," Deborah told Cassandra. "What's more, all of our U-2 stealth strategic bombers broke down midair. What the hell happened? You are a psychic, right? Tell me what's going on."

"There's a powerful female psychic in Japan," Cassandra answered. "Perhaps her power even surpasses that of Jesus. Neither my clairvoyant viewing power, remote mind control, nor remote force works on the woman. She must be one of God's most powerful protectors."

"You're telling me that a Japanese psychic shot down 300 American ICBMs? I don't believe that. We have the U.S.–Japan alliance, and Russia should be their enemy."

"Well, the Russian military is baffled, too. All 10 hypersonic missiles that Russia shot toward the United States at Mach 20 speed also disappeared. Her powers are godlike," Cassandra said.

"Impossible. Can you change the trajectory of even a single pistol bullet?"

"If I could change the trajectory of a pistol bullet, I would appear in *The Matrix* and earn at least 10 million dollars."

"That's ridiculous," Deborah said. "Then I'll have our Seventh Fleet operate a nuclear submarine and fire eight nuclear missiles throughout Russia. Use your clairvoyance and look carefully where they go, understand?"

Thus, eight nuclear missiles were fired into Khabarovsk, Vladivostok, St. Petersburg, and Moscow, two missiles per city. But again, these eight missiles disappeared from their radar around the time they left the atmosphere.

"It's impossible. Impossible. Do something about it," Deborah said.

"God must despise nuclear weapons," Cassandra answered.

"Fine. Then tell me how many years I have left."

"If I answer that, the CIA will kill me."

"That means the CIA thinks it's easier to eliminate me than to assassinate Rasputin. Fine, that's enough."

Both the secretary of defense and the secretary

of state shrugged their shoulders. Neither President Deborah, President Rasputin, nor America's no. 1 psychic Cassandra was aware that at 100,000 feet above the earth was the space being Yaidron with his fleet of 100 UFOs. They didn't show up on the radar, and they reacted to anything over the speed of Mach 20 with teleportation. To their eyes, an activated ICBM was as slow as a fly; it was way too easy to shoot down an ICBM using their electron guns.

Yaidron, dressed in a blue outfit with an "R" mark on his chest, telepathically informed The-Holy-One in Japan of the situation. The-Holy-One gave a brief response: "Thank you, as always." Yaidron responded, "If you ever need us for a mission, please call us over at any time."

Meanwhile, Agnes was worried that Japan would be forsaken by God's love if it stayed like this. *God will surely bring some kind of divine punishment onto the 125 million Japanese peo-*

ple, who are living selfishly and nonchalantly, seeking only worldly pleasures, without knowing good from evil, heaven from hell, or angels from devils, she thought.

The Great Hanshin-Awaji earthquake on January 17, 1995, effectively kept Japan from enjoying further development and prosperity. Thousands of people died, but the Japanese did not increase their faith.

On March 11, 2011, nearly 20,000 lives were lost to the Great East Japan Earthquake and the following massive tsunami, but even at that time, the people didn't strengthen their faith in God at all. Instead, when some people claimed the natural disaster to be "God's punishment" or "Buddha's punishment," the Japanese shouted verbal abuse at them, saying they lacked awareness for human rights. Then, people's hatred turned to nuclear power plants and global warming.

When the coronavirus spread all over the

world, only the "vaccination totalitarianism" prevailed; infectious disease experts who pandered to the government were regarded in a manner akin to "agents of God," and hospitals replaced religious temples as the "modern shrine." People were starting to become like ants that would be supervised by artificial intelligence (AI). There was no room for faith in God in an AI-surveillance-based democracy. Japan was rapidly being Sinicized.

When President Donald King of America shouted, "Keep the church doors open even if COVID spreads!" the media, which believed themselves to be the gods of democracy, mocked the president; the people also booed him for being unscientific.

We can't keep going like this, Agnes thought. *Something much more terrifying is bound to happen.* Agnes' soul was anticipating the next great crisis.

Then, Mt. Fuji erupted for the first time in 300 years. Solar panels stopped functioning from the ashfall. The sky above Nagoya and Tokyo turned gray and cloudy with ashes. *Next up will be a great earthquake in the Tokyo metropolitan region, I'm sure. For the first time in 100 years, Tokyo will be hit by a magnitude-9.0 earthquake, followed by a tsunami.* Agnes decided to leave everything in the hands of God residing in heaven.

17.

The day finally came.

Three days after Mr. Fuji erupted for the first time in 300 years, a great epicentral earthquake hit Japan's capital, Tokyo. An earthquake measuring "upper 6" on the Japanese seismic intensity scale wouldn't usually inflict much damage to Tokyo, but the earthquake on that day began with three vertical shakings, followed by five lengthy consecutive waves of horizontal, swing-like shakings. The official seismic intensity measurement was never announced because the Meteorological Agency building had utterly collapsed. Tokyo Tower, the second tower, and Shibuya Scramble Square Tower collapsed as well. NHK, which had been undergoing reconstruction, crumbled yet again, so blue tents marked "NHK" with a thick marker lined up along Yoyogi Park.

This time, TV Asahi in Roppongi Hills wasn't safe either. The gods of Japan had always hated left-wing broadcasting.

CNN and BBC made arbitrary assessments on Japan's seismic intensity. They reported that it was a magnitude-9.0 earthquake, or above upper 7 on the Japanese seismic intensity scale.

This earthquake that struck during the early morning rush hour was estimated to have killed over two million people. The damage had spread throughout the Tokyo metropolitan area, and it would take a week to assess the overall extent of the destruction.

Moreover, a massive tsunami hit Tokyo just as the high tide came in after lunchtime. There were no such things as tall buildings anymore, and all the low-rise buildings sank to the bottom of the water.

Rumors went around that this earthquake was 100 times larger and more intense than the Great

East Japan Earthquake, but there were no newspaper companies left in the Tokyo metropolitan area that could issue a newspaper extra to report on the earthquake.

TV and newspapers in western Japan gradually unraveled the facts. For the people of Tokyo, this day was close to being the last day of humankind. Japan had lost its brain.

Agnes climbed to the roof right above the third floor of a sheltered apartment in Ikedayama. Many areas of Tokyo were zero feet above sea level, so downtown Tokyo had been swallowed by the muddy waters and turned into a lake.

Here, Ikedayama sat on an elevation of more than 100 feet, and the rooftop was more than 130 feet above sea level. It could take a few days for the water to recede, but just as expected from an ex-dormitory for Supreme Court judges, the building did not collapse even though its walls cracked. Rubber boats were already sent out near

Gotanda Station.

All of a sudden, Agnes heard the sound of a helicopter from above.

Vice-Minister Manobe and Assistant Director Kazumi Suzumoto came down to the rooftop.

"Ms. Agnes, are you alright?" Manobe asked.

"Yes. The tsunami didn't exceed 100 feet," Agnes answered.

"I was told in advance by The-Holy-One to keep you in a shelter that is at least 100 feet above sea level," Suzumoto said.

"It may take a month to recover, but at least the volcanic ashes were washed away," Manobe said. "Tokyo Tower and the second tower were destroyed, but electricity hasn't been restored yet in the first place. We're discussing with the Ministry of Land, Infrastructure, Transport, and Tourism to reorganize utility poles and power lines using this opportunity. It's inconvenient for helicopters to take off and land if there are too many power lines."

Manobe had seriously anticipated that the entire city of Tokyo could be hit by nuclear missiles and turned into a sea of fire, so he was prepared to accept any damage. But now, he was glad that he had sent the Maritime Self-Defense Force out to the sea in advance; that meant they still had military capabilities. He was also happy that he was still able to mobilize the Self-Defense Forces stationed in the northern Tokyo metropolitan district and northern Japan.

Agnes thought about how much damage the Japanese economy would suffer. She also felt that natural disasters around the world were just beginning. As she gazed out at the flooded area in the central part of great Tokyo, Agnes pondered how many similar incidents had occurred in past civilizations.

Meanwhile, Manobe thought that Japan would not be involved in any international nuclear warfare for the time being, thanks to the news of the massive earthquake. *A new political leader will surely emerge*, he thought. *The coronavirus, a world war, a great earthquake, and a great tsunami. The U.S. government said they would offer military assistance to rescue Japan, so they will probably go from a kill-people mode to a help-people mode. People find friendship in misfortune, but they often become self-centered and selfish in the midst of happiness. No one thinks about God and Buddha during a battle for hegemony, but after a catastrophe, there will be more people with pure hearts—those who believe in God and Buddha.*

"The-Holy-One is saying he'll soon stop the eruption of Mt. Fuji," Manobe said. "Apparently, he still has important work to do, and he expects Agnes to help him."

"Does this pretty lady in her 20s have to continuously be nailed to the cross?" asked Chief Yamane, who was protecting Agnes, looking slightly fatigued.

"Guns and aikido are useless against a great earthquake. It hit me just how powerless I am," murmured Haruka Kazami.

"Who knows if we can even secure food," Chiemi Anzai complained. "All this time, I thought we were the ones protecting this town, but it turned out that only when the town was peaceful could police activities be carried out. Most convenience stores were facing the streets, so they sank. All I can think about right now are instant stir-fried noodles and instant ramen. We'll have to live on candles at night. I doubt electricity will be restored for a while."

"I'm proud of myself for having successfully protected Ms. Agnes amid this great earthquake and tsunami. Our job is to continue to keep her safe," Kazuo Minegishi said.

"Ms. Kazumi Suzumoto, you've already thought about securing our essentials, right?" Susumu Takarada winked at her.

"Yes. After all, the Self-Defense Forces take logistics very seriously. At any rate, I'll prepare essential supplies by tonight," Suzumoto said. All Secret Service team loosened up with relief.

18.

That day, Agnes was sent to the top of Mt. Soun in Hakone on the Self-Defense Forces' helicopter. The-Holy-One was already standing there, arms crossed, in his kimono.

In Shizuoka Prefecture, too, there was a stream of pyroclastic flow pouring into the ocean.

The same was true in Kanagawa Prefecture. Mt. Fuji spewed volcanic bombs from time to time, and volcanic gas was covering the entire sky.

Although Agnes was meeting with The-Holy-One for the first time, she felt like she had known him from long ago. She recalled the emotions she felt when she met the Lord God in heaven; this made her heart race, and a rush of blood made her blush.

The-Holy-One opened his arms wide and spoke briefly: "Watch carefully the work of your Father."

"O God Ame-no-Mioya-Gami, the oldest God of Japan who descended from Andromeda Galaxy unto this land of Yamato 30,000 years ago. May you revive your power. And once more, show China your power that once chased out barbarian Chinese tribes, as Giant God Pan Gu."

Saying so, The-Holy-One turned his palms up and raised his arms. A rumbling roar echoed from the Gora district; it was as if the earth was violently heaving upward. Everything was blown away, from the row of inns to the railways in the Gora district. The hard base of the earth that was like a turtle's shell cracked into smaller pieces, and a streamlined, gigantic spaceship that was several hundred feet long came up to the surface. The ship's body was glistening in black, and small spherical electric objects were attached onto the hull, flashing lightning in all directions.

A fleet of about 1,000 UFOs filled the sky above the gigantic spaceship. Several F-35 jets of the Self-Defense Forces scrambled but quickly retreated to their bases after seeing the majesty of the spaceship.

The flagship, *Andromeda Galaxy*, was at least 2,600 feet long and 650 feet wide. Nearby, protector UFOs headed by space beings Yaidron, R. A. Goal, and Metatron, each about 650 feet in diameter, guarded the great ship.

A UFO was sent from the flagship to Mt. Soun. The UFO looked like a flying saucer, and it was about 100 feet in diameter. The UFO landed, the hatch opened, and a translucent staircase came down automatically. The-Holy-One—yes, El Cantare—and Agnes took one step on the staircase, and another. Then, the stairs automatically pulled them into the ship and the hatch closed. The UFO they had just entered was sucked into the flagship, *Andromeda Galaxy*, which was floating midair. The two of them were led to a room with a large monitor that looked like an observation deck. All the caretakers were androids modeled after Japanese women.

Agnes looked to her right and saw that The-Holy-One had on different clothing before she knew it—a navy blue outfit with an *R.O.* mark on his chest. Agnes realized that she, too, wore a pink outfit with the *R.O.* mark on her chest.

"Let's go." The flagship UFO rose even higher into the atmosphere. Mt. Fuji got smaller and smaller.

El Cantare spoke.

"Thirty thousand years ago, we landed on the Second Fuji that existed right beside Mt. Fuji. And we created a new civilization in this country. The civilization spread to China and the Korean Peninsula, enlightening the people there, and it guided India and the legendary Mu Empire to prosperity."

"I remember that. I called you 'Father' at the time," Agnes said.

El Cantare chuckled and said, "Shall we begin?"

On the monitor, islands surfaced one by one on the Pacific side of Japan. Then, a new continent began to rise above the waters leading to Indonesia. This continent seemed to be about the size of Australia.

"It's the new continent of Mu," he said. "I was born as the Mu Empire's Great King of Light, Ra Mu, 16,000 years ago."

"That's so widely known that even I know it," Agnes said.

"But after that, the Mu civilization plunged into deism for 1,000 years. People came to deny all mystical phenomena and ideas, and anything other than rationality and reason was deemed to be unrealistic."

Agnes nodded.

"Then, the continent sank in three stages."

"Another story goes that the civilization sank overnight."

The-Holy-One continued.

"If the country of Japan continues like this, and if atheism, materialism, scientism, and the wrong tradition that began with Kant—the idea that anything beyond human reason is neither academic nor truthful—are to continue prevailing on the Earth, I must destroy this Seventh Civilization. I've decided to save only those with righteous minds. I will only allow those souls to reincarnate. This Earth shall be purified."

"Watch closely what is about to happen, Agnes. The Seventh Civilization will die out and the Eighth Civilization will be born."

Agnes glued her eyes to the monitor.

The monitor showed that the United States of America began to sink into the sea, starting with the west coast. Along with countless nuclear weapons, the last leader nation of the Earth civilization perished. On the monitor, Agnes saw President Deborah floating between ocean waves until she was eventually eaten by sharks.

Meanwhile, the New Atlantis continent rose up around the waters of Bermuda. A group of people who open-mindedly accepted God's revelations made their way over to New Atlantis.

Russia also began to sink into the ocean—especially places that held nuclear weapon silos. Glaciers in the Arctic Ocean melted, and the water gushed into the Russian land. Even President Rasputin and his aides sank deep below the ocean as they prayed in their cathedral.

In the E.U., hail crushed building after building with powerful force. Later, fireballs showered across the E.U. like rain and storm. The E.U. and Great Britain sank into the ocean without leaving any trace of civilization.

In Africa, an enormous storm of flames broke out and burned all land. In the Islamic regions from Africa to the Middle East, desperate people called the name of Allah in their mosques, but there was nothing that could be done, as Allah Himself was the one creating their havoc. Allah didn't forgive Islam for its never-ending terrorism. The Indian subcontinent, Pakistan, and Central Asia were also swept away by a massive tsunami; they sank into the ocean, leaving behind only the Himalayan Mountains.

Many polytheistic religions in India were low-level, and the Lord God did not allow for their continued existence.

The Lord God had no intention to overlook the regions with never-ending war: Israel, Palestine, Iran, and Iraq. Enough hailstorms and fireballs fell onto the regions until the civilization sank into the sea.

The Lord God allowed the emergence of the legendary Lemuria Continent in the Indian Ocean. People with pure hearts, along with their souls, were given the chance to live on this land as human beings.

Similarly, Central and South America were hit by enormous earthquakes, volcanic explosions, and great tsunamis. Their civilization went down, leaving only mountains behind.

"Now," he said, as the enormous UFO and its fleet moved to the sky above China.

El Cantare spoke.

"The Chinese civilization and the civilization of the Korean Peninsula are hopeless beyond saving. I have made my decision. They shall be destroyed."

A gigantic cross-shaped rift valley appeared over the Chinese continent, and the 700 million people, who once survived, were swallowed into seawater.

The Korean Peninsula disappeared from the earth.

The-Holy-One looked back at Agnes and asked, "Now, what would you like to do with Japan?"

"As You wish," Agnes answered.

Hail and fireballs rained down on urban cities throughout the Japanese archipelago.

Hundreds and thousands of lightning strikes occurred.

"The ones surviving shall establish a civilization on the new continent of Mu."

And thus the world map was redrawn quite drastically.

New Atlantis, New Mu, New Lemuria, Australia, and old civilizations that were left on separate islands—these would be the beginning of the Eighth Civilization.

"Father, it should be enough," Agnes said.

"You may be right," El Cantare said.

"What shall we do next?"

"We will expel malicious space beings that are nesting on the dark side of the Moon and on Mars. Then, why don't we return to the Andromeda Galaxy for the time being?" El Cantare said.

"But in 1,000 years, let's come back here to see how things are going," Agnes said.

"You shall become a new god at that time," El Cantare told her.

The universe was infinitely vast.

I must inspect other Messiah planets once we return to the Andromeda Galaxy.

The mother ship carrying El Cantare warped off into infinity.

End of the story.

19.

The Pacific Ocean was infinitely vast and abundant with water. A man and a woman were sharing a rubber boat.

"How long do I need to keep rowing until we reach a new continent?" the man asked.

"Strength and stamina are your strong suits, so row until you die. We're out of canned crab, so if you die first, I'll slice your body like raw fish and eat it. This survival knife here will come in handy," the woman said.

"Is there no such thing as love or compassion in your dictionary?"

"Anyway, even if we reach some island, we won't have jobs."

"I'll become the Adam of the new age, and you can be Eve. Together, we'll start a new age. What do you say? Isn't that romantic?"

"Hm, how 'bout you become prime minister and I'll be chief cabinet secretary?"

"We've got no citizens."

"We'll order all living creatures on whatever-island to be our 'people.'"

"Maybe we'll stick to being cops and arrest snakes and monkeys."

The two of them were Chief Naoyuki Yamane of the Metropolitan Police Department's First Criminal Investigation Division and Chief Haruka Kazami of the Public Security Bureau.

Just then, a small black hole appeared in the sky.

A white dove flew out.

The dove dropped a white envelope it was carrying in its beak onto the rubber boat. The envelope contained a handwritten letter.

Dear Chief Yamane:

Knowing you, I am sure you have survived through those crises. Ever since I left you, I fought alongside Lord El Cantare to defeat malicious aliens on the dark side of the Moon and on Mars—the very perpetrators that put the Earth in turmoil. Then, we returned to Andromeda Galaxy. I was welcomed by many familiar faces. Now, I am self-reflecting on whether I myself could truly fulfill my duty as one of the Seraphim.

I could not save the Earth. But although the Seventh Civilization of the Earth fell, I believe the new Eighth Civilization is on the rise. It should be about 1,000 years, our time, but perhaps about one month, your time. I was given permission to be reborn on the New Continent of Mu. My duty as a savior is still incomplete. Please wait for me, Archangel Gabriel. The real reconstruction begins soon.

Agnes

The letter ended there.

It was like blessed rain after a drought.

It was "Good News" that the new wheels would soon begin to turn.

How will the new civilization turn out?

Will it become a civilization where angels can make their appearances?

Yamane's heart was filled with new hope while Kazami poked him from behind.

THE END

ABOUT THE AUTHOR

Founder and CEO of Happy Science Group.

Ryuho Okawa was born on July 7th 1956, in Tokushima, Japan. After graduating from the University of Tokyo with a law degree, he joined a Tokyo-based trading house. While working at its New York headquarters, he studied international finance at the Graduate Center of the City University of New York. In 1981, he attained Great Enlightenment and became aware that he is El Cantare with a mission to bring salvation to all humankind.

In 1986, he established Happy Science. It now has members in over 165 countries across the world, with more than 700 branches and temples as well as 10,000 missionary houses around the world.

He has given over 3,450 lectures (of which more than 150 are in English) and published over 3,000 books (of which more than 600 are Spiritual Interview Series), and many are translated into 40 languages. Along with *The Laws of the Sun* and *The Laws Of Messiah*, many of the books have become best sellers or million sellers. To date, Happy Science has produced 25 movies. The original story and original concept were given by the Executive Producer Ryuho Okawa. He has also composed music and written lyrics of over 450 pieces.

Moreover, he is the Founder of Happy Science University and Happy Science Academy (Junior and Senior High School), Founder and President of the Happiness Realization Party, Founder and Honorary Headmaster of Happy Science Institute of Government and Management, Founder of IRH Press Co., Ltd., and the Chairperson of NEW STAR PRODUCTION Co., Ltd. and ARI Production Co., Ltd.

WHAT IS EL CANTARE?

El Cantare means "the Light of the Earth," and is the Supreme God of the Earth who has been guiding humankind since the beginning of Genesis. He is whom Jesus called Father and Muhammad called Allah, and is *Ame-no-Mioya-Gami*, Japanese Father God. Different parts of El Cantare's core consciousness have descended to Earth in the past, once as Alpha and another as Elohim. His branch spirits, such as Shakyamuni Buddha and Hermes, have descended to Earth many times and helped to flourish many civilizations. To unite various religions and to integrate various fields of study in order to build a new civilization on Earth, a part of the core consciousness has descended to Earth as Master Ryuho Okawa.

Alpha is a part of the core consciousness of El Cantare who descended to Earth around 330 million years ago. Alpha preached Earth's Truths to harmonize and unify Earth-born humans and space people who came from other planets.

Elohim is a part of El Cantare's core consciousness who descended to Earth around 150 million years ago. He gave wisdom, mainly on the differences of light and darkness, good and evil.

Ame-no-Mioya-Gami (Japanese Father God) is the Creator God and the Father God who appears in the ancient literature, *Hotsuma Tsutae*. It is believed that He descended on the foothills of Mt. Fuji about 30,000 years ago and built the Fuji dynasty, which is the root of the Japanese civilization. With justice as the central pillar, Ame-no-Mioya-Gami's teachings spread to ancient civilizations of other countries in the world.

Shakyamuni Buddha was born as a prince into the Shakya Clan in India around 2,600 years ago. When he was 29 years old, he renounced the world and sought enlightenment. He later attained Great Enlightenment and founded Buddhism.

Hermes is one of the 12 Olympian gods in Greek mythology, but the spiritual Truth is that he taught the teachings of love and progress around 4,300 years ago that became the origin of the current Western civilization. He is a hero that truly existed.

Ophealis was born in Greece around 6,500 years ago and was the leader who took an expedition to as far as Egypt. He is the God of miracles, prosperity, and arts, and is known as Osiris in the Egyptian mythology.

Rient Arl Croud was born as a king of the ancient Incan Empire around 7,000 years ago and taught about the mysteries of the mind. In the heavenly world, he is responsible for the interactions that take place between various planets.

Thoth was an almighty leader who built the golden age of the Atlantic civilization around 12,000 years ago. In the Egyptian mythology, he is known as god Thoth.

Ra Mu was a leader who built the golden age of the civilization of Mu around 17,000 years ago. As a religious leader and a politician, he ruled by uniting religion and politics.

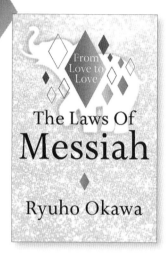

The 28th Laws Series

From Love to Love

The Laws Of
Messiah

Ryuho Okawa

The Laws Of Messiah
From Love to Love

Paperback • 248 pages • $16.95
ISBN: 978-1-942125-90-7 (Jan. 31, 2022)

"What is Messiah?" This book carries an important message of love and guidance to people living now from the Modern-Day Messiah or the Modern-Day Savior. It also reveals the secret of Shambhala, the spiritual center of Earth, as well as the truth that this spiritual center is currently in danger of perishing and what we can do to protect this sacred place.

Love your Lord God. Know that those who don't know love don't know God. Discover the true love of God and the ideal practice of faith. This book teaches the most important element we must not lose sight of as we go through our soul training on this planet Earth.

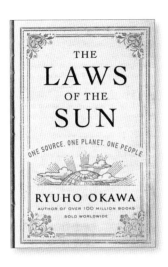

THE LAWS OF THE SUN

ONE SOURCE, ONE PLANET, ONE PEOPLE

Paperback • 288 pages • $15.95
ISBN: 978-1-942125-43-3 (Oct. 15, 2018)

Imagine if you could ask God why he created this world and what spiritual laws he used to shape us—and everything around us. In *The Laws of the Sun*, Ryuho Okawa outlines these laws of the universe and provides a road map for living one's life with greater purpose and meaning. This powerful book shows the way to realize true happiness—a happiness that continues from this world through the other.

DISCOVER THE TRUTH BEHIND THE MYSTERY

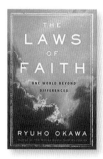

THE LAWS OF FAITH

ONE WORLD BEYOND DIFFERENCES

Paperback • 208 pages • $15.95
ISBN: 978-1-942125-34-1 (Mar. 31, 2018)

Ryuho Okawa preaches at the core of a new universal religion from various angles while integrating logical and spiritual viewpoints in mind with current world situations. This book offers us the key to accept diversities beyond differences to create a world filled with peace and prosperity.

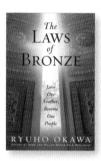

THE LAWS OF BRONZE

LOVE ONE ANOTHER, BECOME ONE PEOPLE

Paperback • 224 pages • $15.95
ISBN: 978-1-942125-50-1 (Mar. 15, 2019)

This is the 25th volume of the Laws Series by Ryuho Okawa. This miraculous and inspiring book will show the keys to living a spiritual life of truth regardless of their age, gender, or race.

R. A. GOAL'S WORDS FOR THE FUTURE

MESSAGES FROM A SPACE BEING
TO THE PEOPLE OF EARTH

Paperback • $11.95 • ISBN: 978-1-943928-10-1
E-book • $10.99 • ISBN: 978-1-943928-11-8

R. A. Goal, a certified messiah from Planet Andalucia Beta in Ursa Minor, gives humans on Earth three predictions for 2021. They include the prospect of the novel coronavirus pandemic, the outlook of economic crisis, and the risk of war. But the hope is that Savior is now born on Earth to overcome any bad predictions. Now is the time to open our hearts and listen to the words from R. A. Goal.

THE DESCENT OF JAPANESE FATHER GOD AME-NO-MIOYA-GAMI

THE "GOD OF CREATION" IN THE ANCIENT DOCUMENT *HOTSUMA TSUTAE*

Paperback • $14.95 • ISBN: 978-1-943928-29-3
E-book • $13.99 • ISBN: 978-1-943928-31-6

By reading this book, you can find the origin of bushido (samurai spirit) and understand how the ancient Japanese civilization influenced other countries. Now that the world is in confusion, Japan is expected to awaken to its true origin and courageously rise to bring justice to the world.

SPIRITUAL MESSAGES FROM METATRON LIGHT IN THE TIMES OF CRISIS

Paperback • 146 pages • $11.95
ISBN: 978-1-943928-19-4 (Nov. 4, 2021)

Metatron is one of the highest-ranked angels (Seraphim) in Judaism and Christianity, and also one of the saviors of universe who has guided the civilizations of many planets including Earth, under the guidance of Lord God. Such savior has sent a message upon seeing the crisis of Earth. You will also learn about the truth behind the coronavirus pandemic, the unimaginable extent of China's desire, the danger of appeasement policy toward China, and the secret of Metatron.

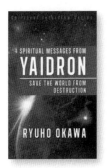

SPIRITUAL MESSAGES FROM YAIDRON SAVE THE WORLD FROM DESTRUCTION

Paperback • $11.95 • ISBN: 978-1-943928-23-1
E-book • $10.99 • ISBN: 978-1-943928-25-5

In this book, Yaidron explains what was going on behind the military coup in Myanmar and Taliban's control over Afghanistan. He also warns of the imminent danger approaching Taiwan. What is now going on is a battle between democratic values and the communist one-party control. How to overcome this battle and create peace on Earth depends on the faith and righteous actions of each one of us.

The Unknown Stigma Series

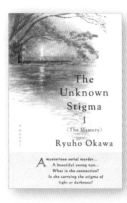

Published on October 1, 2022

The Unknown Stigma 1
\<The Mystery\>

Hardcover • 192 pages • $17.95
ISBN: 978-1-942125-28-0

The first spiritual mystery novel by Ryuho Okawa. It happened one early summer afternoon, in a densely wooded park in Tokyo: following a loud scream of a young woman, the alleged victim was found lying with his eyes rolled back and foaming at the mouth. But there was no sign of forced trauma, nor even a drop of blood. Then, similar murder cases continued one after another without any clues. Later, this mysterious serial murder case leads back to a young Catholic nun...

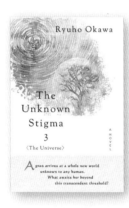

Coming in December 2022

The Unknown Stigma 3
\<The Universe\>

Hardcover • 184 pages • $17.95
ISBN: 978-1-958655-00-9

In this astonishing sequel to the first two installments of *The Unknown Stigma*, the protagonist journeys through the universe and encounters a mystical world unknown to humankind. Discover what awaits her beyond this mysterious world.

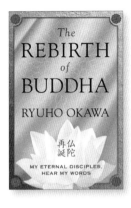

Published on August 15, 2022

THE REBIRTH OF BUDDHA

MY ETERNAL DISCIPLES,
HEAR MY WORDS

Paperback • 280 pages • $17.95
ISBN: 978-1-942125-95-2

These are the messages of Buddha who has returned to this modern age as promised to His eternal beloved disciples. They are in simple words and poetic style, yet contain profound messages. Once you start reading these passages, your soul will be replenished as the plant absorbs the water, and you will remember why you chose this era to be born into with Buddha. Listen to the voices of your Eternal Master and awaken to your calling.

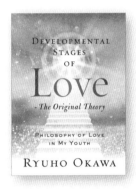

Published on June 15, 2022

DEVELOPMENTAL STAGES OF LOVE - THE ORIGINAL THEORY

PHILOSOPHY OF LOVE IN MY YOUTH

Hardcover • 200 pages • $17.95
ISBN: 978-1-942125-94-5

This book is about author Ryuho Okawa's original philosophy of love which serves as the foundation of love in the chapter three of *The Laws of the Sun*. It consists of series of short essays authored during his age of 25 through 28 while he was working as a young promising business elite at an international trading company after attaining the Great Enlightenment in 1981. The developmental stages of love unites love and enlightenment, West and East, and bridges Christianity and Buddhism.

THE SPIRITUAL TRUTH

2021 No. 1 bestseller in all categories by Tohan, Japan

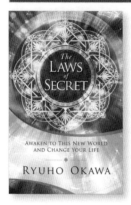

THE LAWS OF SECRET

AWAKEN TO THIS NEW WORLD AND CHANGE YOUR LIFE

Paperback • 248 pages • $16.95
ISBN: 978-1-942125-81-5 (Apr. 20, 2021)

Our physical world coexists with the multi-dimensional spirit world and we are constantly interacting with some kind of spiritual energy, whether positive or negative, without consciously realizing it. This book reveals how our lives are affected by invisible influences, including the spiritual reasons behind influenza, the novel coronavirus infection, and other illnesses. The new view of the world in this book will inspire you to change your life in a better direction, and to become someone who can give hope and courage to others in this age of confusion.

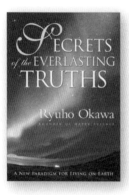

SECRETS OF THE EVERLASTING TRUTHS

A NEW PARADIGM FOR LIVING ON EARTH

Paperback • 144 pages • $14.95
ISBN: 978-1-937673-10-9 (Jun. 16, 2012)

Okawa offers a glimpse of the vast universe created by God and discloses that humanity is intimately guided by celestial influences. Our planet will experience a decisive paradigm shift of "knowledge" and "truth," culminating in an era of paradoxical spirituality, where mastery of science will depend on spiritual knowledge. The advancement that we seek, resides within us.

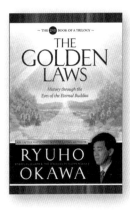

THE GOLDEN LAWS

HISTORY THROUGH THE EYES OF THE ETERNAL BUDDHA

E-book • 201 pages • $13.99
ISBN: 978-1-941779-82-8 (Jul. 1, 2011)

Throughout history, Great Guiding Spirits have been present on Earth in both the East and the West at crucial points in human history to further our spiritual development. *The Golden Laws* reveals how Divine Plan has been unfolding on Earth, and outlines 5,000 years of the secret history of humankind. Once we understand the true course of history, through past, present and into the future, we cannot help but become aware of the significance of our spiritual mission in the present age.

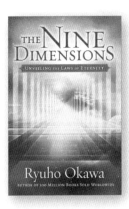

THE NINE DIMENSIONS

UNVEILING THE LAWS OF ETERNITY

Paperback • 168 pages • $15.95
ISBN: 978-0-982698-56-3 (Feb. 16, 2012)

This book is a window into the mind of our loving God, who designed this world and the vast, wondrous world of our afterlife as a school with many levels through which our souls learn and grow. When the religions and cultures of the world discover the truth of their common spiritual origin, they will be inspired to accept their differences, come together under faith in God, and build an era of harmony and peaceful progress on Earth.

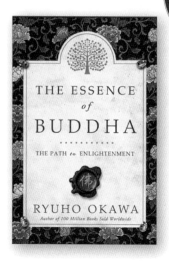

THE ESSENCE OF BUDDHA

THE PATH TO ENLIGHTENMENT

Paperback • 208 pages • $14.95
ISBN: 978-1-942125-06-8 (Oct.1, 2016)

In this book, Ryuho Okawa imparts in simple and accessible language his wisdom about the essence of Shakyamuni Buddha's philosophy of life and enlightenment-teachings that have been inspiring people all over the world for over 2,500 years. By offering a new perspective on core Buddhist thoughts that have long been cloaked in mystique, Okawa brings these teachings to life for modern people. *The Essence of Buddha* distills a way of life that anyone can practice to achieve a life of self-growth, compassionate living, and true happiness.

THE TEN PRINCIPLES FROM EL CANTARE VOLUME I

RYUHO OKAWA'S FIRST LECTURES ON HIS BASIC TEACHINGS

Paperback • 232 pages • $16.95
ISBN: 978-1-942125-85-3 (Dec. 15, 2021)

This book contains the historic lectures given on the first five principles of the Ten Principles of Happy Science from the author, Ryuho Okawa, who is revered as World Teacher. These lectures produced an enthusiastic fellowship in Happy Science Japan and became the foundation of the current global utopian movement. You can learn the essence of Okawa's teachings and the secret behind the rapid growth of the Happy Science movement in simple language.

THE TEN PRINCIPLES FROM EL CANTARE VOLUME II

RYUHO OKAWA'S FIRST LECTURES ON HIS WISH TO SAVE THE WORLD

Paperback • 272 pages • $16.95
ISBN: 978-1-942125-86-0 (May. 3, 2022)

A sequel to *The Ten Principles from El Cantare Volume I*. Volume II reveals the Creator's three major inventions; the secret of the creation of human souls, the meaning of time, and 'happiness' as life's purpose. By reading this book, you can not only improve yourself but learn how to make differences in society and create an ideal, utopian world.

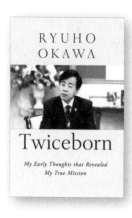

TWICEBORN

MY EARLY THOUGHTS THAT REVEALED MY TRUE MISSION

Hardcover • 206 pages • $19.95
ISBN: 978-1-942125-74-7 (Oct. 7, 2020)

This semi-autobiography of Ryuho Okawa reveals the origins of his thoughts and how he made up his mind to establish Happy Science to spread the Truth to the world. It also contains the very first grand lecture where he declared himself as El Cantare. The timeless wisdom in Twiceborn will surely inspire you and help you fulfill your mission in this lifetime.

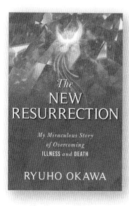

THE NEW RESURRECTION

MY MIRACULOUS STORY OF OVERCOMING ILLNESS AND DEATH

Hardcover • 224 pages • $19.95
ISBN: 978-1-942125-64-8 (Feb. 26, 2020)

The New Resurrection is an autobiographical account of an astonishing miracle experienced by author Ryuho Okawa in 2004. This event was adapted into the feature-length film *Immortal Hero*. Today, Okawa lives each day with the readiness to die for the Truth and has dedicated his life to selflessly guiding faith seekers towards spiritual development and happiness.

OTHER RECOMMENDED TITLES

For a complete list of books, visit <u>okawabooks.com</u>

MUSIC BY RYUHO OKAWA

El Cantare Ryuho Okawa Original Songs

A song celebrating Lord God

A song celebrating Lord God, the God of the Earth, who is beyond a prophet.

DVD
CD

The Water Revolution

English and Chinese version

For the truth and happiness of the 1.4 billion people in China who have no freedom. Love, justice, and sacred rage of God are on this melody that will give you courage to fight to bring peace.

DVD

CD

Search on YouTube

 the water revolution 🔍 for a short ad!

Listen now today!

 Download from
Spotify iTunes Amazon

DVD, CD available at amazon.com, and Happy Science locations worldwide

With Savior *English version*

DVD

This is the message of hope to the modern people who are living in the midst of the Coronavirus pandemic, natural disasters, economic depression, and other various crises.

Search on YouTube

| with savior 🔍 | for a short ad!

CD

The Thunder

a composition for repelling the Coronavirus

We have been granted this music from our Lord. It will repel away the novel Coronavirus originated in China. Experience this magnificent powerful music.

Search on YouTube

| the thunder composition 🔍 |

for a short ad!

CD

The Exorcism

prayer music for repelling Lost Spirits

Feel the divine vibrations of this Japanese and Western exorcising symphony to banish all evil possessions you suffer from and to purify your space!

Search on YouTube

| the exorcism repelling 🔍 |

for a short ad!

CD

Listen now today!

 Download from
Spotify iTunes Amazon

DVD, CD available at amazon.com, and Happy Science locations worldwide

ABOUT HAPPY SCIENCE

Happy Science is a global movement that empowers individuals to find purpose and spiritual happiness and to share that happiness with their families, societies, and the world. With more than 12 million members around the world, Happy Science aims to increase awareness of spiritual truths and expand our capacity for love, compassion, and joy so that together we can create the kind of world we all wish to live in.

Activities at Happy Science are based on the Principle of Happiness (Love, Wisdom, Self-Reflection, and Progress). This principle embraces worldwide philosophies and beliefs, transcending boundaries of culture and religions.

Love teaches us to give ourselves freely without expecting anything in return; it encompasses giving, nurturing, and forgiving.

Wisdom leads us to the insights of spiritual truths, and opens us to the true meaning of life and the will of God (the universe, the highest power, Buddha).

Self-Reflection brings a mindful, nonjudgmental lens to our thoughts and actions to help us find our truest selves—the essence of our souls—and deepen our connection to the highest power. It helps us attain a clean and peaceful mind and leads us to the right life path.

Progress emphasizes the positive, dynamic aspects of our spiritual growth—actions we can take to manifest and spread happiness around the world. It's a path that not only expands our soul growth, but also furthers the collective potential of the world we live in.

PROGRAMS AND EVENTS

The doors of Happy Science are open to all. We offer a variety of programs and events, including self-exploration and self-growth programs, spiritual seminars, meditation and contemplation sessions, study groups, and book events.

Our programs are designed to:
* Deepen your understanding of your purpose and meaning in life
* Improve your relationships and increase your capacity to love unconditionally
* Attain peace of mind, decrease anxiety and stress, and feel positive
* Gain deeper insights and a broader perspective on the world
* Learn how to overcome life's challenges
    ... and much more.

For more information, visit <u>happy-science.org</u>.

CONTACT INFORMATION

Happy Science is a worldwide organization with branches and temples around the globe. For a comprehensive list, visit the worldwide directory at *happy-science.org*. The following are some of the many Happy Science locations:

UNITED STATES AND CANADA

New York
79 Franklin St., New York, NY 10013, USA
Phone: 1-212-343-7972
Fax: 1-212-343-7973
Email: ny@happy-science.org
Website: happyscience-usa.org

New Jersey
66 Hudson St., #2R, Hoboken, NJ 07030, USA
Phone: 1-201-313-0127
Email: nj@happy-science.org
Website: happyscience-usa.org

Chicago
2300 Barrington Rd., Suite #400,
Hoffman Estates, IL 60169, USA
Phone: 1-630-937-3077
Email: chicago@happy-science.org
Website: happyscience-usa.org

Florida
5208 8th St., Zephyrhills, FL 33542, USA
Phone: 1-813-715-0000
Fax: 1-813-715-0010
Email: florida@happy-science.org
Website: happyscience-usa.org

Atlanta
1874 Piedmont Ave., NE Suite 360-C
Atlanta, GA 30324, USA
Phone: 1-404-892-7770
Email: atlanta@happy-science.org
Website: happyscience-usa.org

San Francisco
525 Clinton St.
Redwood City, CA 94062, USA
Phone & Fax: 1-650-363-2777
Email: sf@happy-science.org
Website: happyscience-usa.org

Los Angeles
1590 E. Del Mar Blvd., Pasadena, CA 91106, USA
Phone: 1-626-395-7775
Fax: 1-626-395-7776
Email: la@happy-science.org
Website: happyscience-usa.org

Orange County
16541 Gothard St. Suite 104
Huntington Beach, CA 92647
Phone: 1-714-659-1501
Email: oc@happy-science.org
Website: happyscience-usa.org

San Diego
7841 Balboa Ave. Suite #202
San Diego, CA 92111, USA
Phone: 1-626-395-7775
Fax: 1-626-395-7776
E-mail: sandiego@happy-science.org
Website: happyscience-usa.org

Hawaii
Phone: 1-808-591-9772
Fax: 1-808-591-9776
Email: hi@happy-science.org
Website: happyscience-usa.org

Kauai
3343 Kanakolu Street, Suite 5
Lihue, HI 96766, USA
Phone: 1-808-822-7007
Fax: 1-808-822-6007
Email: kauai-hi@happy-science.org
Website: happyscience-usa.org

Toronto
845 The Queensway
Etobicoke, ON M8Z 1N6, Canada
Phone: 1-416-901-3747
Email: toronto@happy-science.org
Website: happy-science.ca

Vancouver
#201-2607 East 49th Avenue,
Vancouver, BC, V5S 1J9, Canada
Phone: 1-604-437-7735
Fax: 1-604-437-7764
Email: vancouver@happy-science.org
Website: happy-science.ca

INTERNATIONAL

Tokyo
1-6-7 Togoshi, Shinagawa,
Tokyo, 142-0041, Japan
Phone: 81-3-6384-5770
Fax: 81-3-6384-5776
Email: tokyo@happy-science.org
Website: happy-science.org

Seoul
74, Sadang-ro 27-gil,
Dongjak-gu, Seoul, Korea
Phone: 82-2-3478-8777
Fax: 82-2-3478-9777
Email: korea@happy-science.org
Website: happyscience-korea.org

London
3 Margaret St.
London, W1W 8RE United Kingdom
Phone: 44-20-7323-9255
Fax: 44-20-7323-9344
Email: eu@happy-science.org
Website: www.happyscience-uk.org

Taipei
No. 89, Lane 155, Dunhua N. Road,
Songshan District, Taipei City 105, Taiwan
Phone: 886-2-2719-9377
Fax: 886-2-2719-5570
Email: taiwan@happy-science.org
Website: happyscience-tw.org

Sydney
516 Pacific Highway, Lane Cove North,
2066 NSW, Australia
Phone: 61-2-9411-2877
Fax: 61-2-9411-2822
Email: sydney@happy-science.org

Kuala Lumpur
No 22A, Block 2, Jalil Link Jalan Jalil
Jaya 2, Bukit Jalil 57000,
Kuala Lumpur, Malaysia
Phone: 60-3-8998-7877
Fax: 60-3-8998-7977
Email: malaysia@happy-science.org
Website: happyscience.org.my

Sao Paulo
Rua. Domingos de Morais 1154,
Vila Mariana, Sao Paulo SP
CEP 04010-100, Brazil
Phone: 55-11-5088-3800
Email: sp@happy-science.org
Website: happyscience.com.br

Kathmandu
Kathmandu Metropolitan City,
Ward No. 15, Ring Road, Kimdol,
Sitapaila Kathmandu, Nepal
Phone: 977-1-427-2931
Email: nepal@happy-science.org

Jundiai
Rua Congo, 447, Jd. Bonfiglioli
Jundiai-CEP, 13207-340, Brazil
Phone: 55-11-4587-5952
Email: jundiai@happy-science.org

Kampala
Plot 877 Rubaga Road, Kampala
P.O. Box 34130 Kampala, UGANDA
Phone: 256-79-4682-121
Email: uganda@happy-science.org

ABOUT HAPPINESS REALIZATION PARTY

The Happiness Realization Party (HRP) was founded in May 2009 by Master Ryuho Okawa as part of the Happy Science Group. HRP strives to improve the Japanese society, based on three basic political principles of "freedom, democracy, and faith," and let Japan promote individual and public happiness from Asia to the world as a leader nation.

1) Diplomacy and Security: Protecting Freedom, Democracy, and Faith of Japan and the World from China's Totalitarianism

Japan's current defense system is insufficient against China's expanding hegemony and the threat of North Korea's nuclear missiles. Japan, as the leader of Asia, must strengthen its defense power and promote strategic diplomacy together with the nations which share the values of freedom, democracy, and faith. Further, HRP aims to realize world peace under the leadership of Japan, the nation with the spirit of religious tolerance.

2) Economy: Early economic recovery through utilizing the "wisdom of the private sector"

Economy has been damaged severely by the novel coronavirus originated in China. Many companies have been forced into bankruptcy or out of business. What is needed for economic recovery now is not subsidies and regulations by the government, but policies which can utilize the "wisdom of the private sector."

For more information, visit en.hr-party.jp

HAPPY SCIENCE ACADEMY
JUNIOR AND SENIOR HIGH SCHOOL

Happy Science Academy Junior and Senior High School is a boarding school founded with the goal of educating the future leaders of the world who can have a big vision, persevere, and take on new challenges.

Currently, there are two campuses in Japan; the Nasu Main Campus in Tochigi Prefecture, founded in 2010, and the Kansai Campus in Shiga Prefecture, founded in 2013.

Nasu Main Campus

Kansai Campus

HAPPY SCIENCE UNIVERSITY

THE FOUNDING SPIRIT AND THE GOAL OF EDUCATION

Based on the founding philosophy of the university, "Exploration of happiness and the creation of a new civilization," education, research and studies will be provided to help students acquire deep understanding grounded in religious belief and advanced expertise with the objectives of producing "great talents of virtue" who can contribute in a broad-ranging way to serving Japan and the international society.

FACULTIES

Faculty of human happiness

Students in this faculty will pursue liberal arts from various perspectives with a multidisciplinary approach, explore and envision an ideal state of human beings and society.

Faculty of successful management

This faculty aims to realize successful management that helps organizations to create value and wealth for society and to contribute to the happiness and the development of management and employees as well as society as a whole.

Faculty of future creation

Students in this faculty study subjects such as political science, journalism, performing arts and artistic expression, and explore and present new political and cultural models based on truth, goodness and beauty.

Faculty of future industry

This faculty aims to nurture engineers who can resolve various issues facing modern civilization from a technological standpoint and contribute to the creation of new industries of the future.

ABOUT IRH PRESS

HS Press is an imprint of IRH Press Co., Ltd. IRH Press Co., Ltd., based in Tokyo, was founded in 1987 as a publishing division of Happy Science. IRH Press publishes religious and spiritual books, journals, magazines and also operates broadcast and film production enterprises. For more information, visit *okawabooks.com*.

Follow us on:

f Facebook: Okawa Books

▶ Youtube: Okawa Books

𝓟 Pinterest: Okawa Books

◉ Instagram: OkawaBooks

🐦 Twitter: Okawa Books

g Goodreads: Ryuho Okawa

——— **NEWSLETTER** ———

To receive book related news, promotions and events, please subscribe to our newsletter below.

𝜚 eepurl.com/bsMeJj

——— **AUDIO / VISUAL MEDIA** ———

YOUTUBE

PODCAST

Introduction of Ryuho Okawa's titles; topics ranging from self-help, current affairs, spirituality, religion, and the universe.